The Sacrifice
Paperback Copyright © 2022 Lorhainne Ekelund
Editor: Talia Leduc

ISBN-13: 978-1998775316

Give feedback on the book at:
lorhainneeckhart@hotmail.com

Twitter: @LEckhart
Facebook: AuthorLorhainneEckhart

Printed in the U.S.A

The Sacrifice

BILLY JO MCCABE MYSTERY
BOOK TEN

LORHAINNE ECKHART

The Billy Jo McCabe Mystery

Nothing As It Seems
Hiding in Plain Sight
The Cold Case
The Trap
Above the Law
The Stranger at the Door
The Children
The Last Stand
The Charity
The Sacrifice

The social worker and the cop, an unlikely couple drawn together on a small, secluded Pacific Northwest island where nothing is as it seems. Protecting the innocent comes at a cost, and what seems to be a sleepy, quiet town is anything but.

The Social Worker

Billy Jo McCabe wants only to help children overcome their troubled lives, as she herself struggles to forget the childhood nightmare she survived. She took sociology and prelaw at the insistence of her adoptive father, Chase McCabe, and learned how to use power tools from her adoptive mother, Rose. She loves reading in the backs of bookstores before tucking the book back on the shelf and slipping out without paying. She has a fondness for peanut butter and dill pickle sandwiches, has a

three-legged cat named Harley, hates running (because
that was all she did as a kid), and secretly binges on
brownies and red wine on the sofa in front of her TV
every Friday night.

She's never been married and has dated only twice. She
visits Chase and Rose when summoned and shows up
dutifully for every holiday with her family, but she has
no siblings to speak of, and she feels a growing resent-
ment for the mother who abandoned her in foster care.
Despite proudly maintaining the same prickly attitude
that nearly landed her behind bars as a kid, she has yet
to speak up to Chase, who interferes in her life too
frequently, ready to fix every problem, whether she
wants him to or not.

One thing no one knows about Billy Jo is that she moved
to Roche Harbor because it's the only clue she has about
the last known whereabouts of the woman who abandoned her.

The Cop

Mark Friessen, son of Jed and Diana Friessen, has
landed accidently in the role of small-town detective, a
position in which he's going nowhere. Nearly married
once, and broken-hearted three times, he's sworn he'll
stay single forever, and he keeps his tattoo of a former
girlfriend as a reminder that only fools fall in love. He's
tall, attractive, and stubborn, and he refuses to live in the
shadow of his two older brothers, Chris and Danny.

As Roche Harbor's youngest detective, he sleeps with a

gun under his pillow. He has a stray dog that won't leave, and he swears that the only two food groups that exist are meat and potatoes. His favorite drink is black coffee in the morning, sugared coffee in the afternoon, and a shot of whiskey in his coffee at night to keep him warm.

****Each book in this series is a complete book, with no cliff-hangers, and can be read as a standalone. However, these books may contain references to situations from earlier books in the series. As with any long book series that focuses on specific characters, their changing relationships, and how their lives continue to unfold, you may find it more enjoyable to read the series in order of publishing, as there will be developments and changes in the relationship dynamics of the core characters.*

Chief Mark Friessen is about to be a family man, with a baby on the way. However, he faces a choice: Either he breaks his word to his wife by taking on a job that will put him in danger, or he stays silent, which would haunt him forever.

Mark lives and dies by his word, and he would do anything for his wife but park his morals and turn his back on those he has sworn to protect, kids and animals, a promise he made to his wife and to himself.

After evidence uncovers a global child trafficking network with ties to his island, Mark is contacted by a secret agency of retired servicemen and cops who ask him to help track down and rescue the children no one is looking for.

The only problem is that Billy Jo is pregnant, and accepting the mission will mean Mark needs to leave her for weeks or months on end. As he struggles with his decision to leave the job he loves and the island that has become his home, he realizes he's at a crossroads. He will need to give everything to save the children, bringing an end to the trafficking of minors, and the elite who prey on them, forever. It's the only way to bring everyone involved to justice.

Yet the kids he's trying to save are not the only ones in danger. When a phone call from home brings everything full circle, Mark's ultimate sacrifice could be Billy Jo and his unborn baby.

CHAPTER
One

There was something about the fall, the cool mornings, the days becoming shorter. It seemed everything was preparing for the cold that would soon be upon them. Mark listened to the crackle of wood as he started the early-morning fire in the woodstove to take the chill out of the air.

Still barefoot after pulling on blue jeans and a navy sweatshirt, he heard the familiar sound of Billy Jo's three-legged cat, Harley, munching on kibble. Lucky, his mutt, and Sarge, a light lab, appeared at the sliding glass door, evidently ready to come in, too. He walked over to the door and opened it, taking in the quiet. He'd left his wife sound asleep.

"That was quick this morning," he said to his dogs. The wind was cold, and the rain was just holding off. A light frost, the first of the season, covered the grass.

A door downstairs clicked, and footsteps came up the stairs just as the coffeemaker beeped. "Good morning, Mark," Gail said, pulling at the tie of her pale green robe, wearing slippers and flannel pajama pants. She leaned down and gave Lucky and Sarge a good petting as Mark filled two dog bowls with kibble.

"Good morning, Gail," he said. "Coffee's ready."

"Oh, I see you started the fire," she said. "Think I'll park myself in front of it with coffee this morning. You know, I feel spoiled, Mark. I get up in the morning and you have coffee ready and the house warm. But I've been thinking I can't live here forever. There's a point where I'll need to go home." She turned over one of the four matching green floral mugs that Billy Jo loved, which were sitting beside the coffeemaker, clean and ready. That was just something his wife did. "You get a coffee yet?" Gail asked as she poured hers in the mug.

"No, not yet," he said. "Pour me one, too, please."

Mark put both dog dishes down on the other side of the island, away from the cat, as Gail filled another mug and set it down there for him. "I take it Billy Jo is still asleep," she said.

"No, I'm awake, and I can smell the coffee. Please pour me one, too," Billy Jo said, emerging from the bedroom. She was in a long nightshirt and wool socks, her blue fluffy housecoat pulled on but wide open over her swollen six-month belly. It appeared for a moment as if the baby had grown overnight. Damn, she was a beautiful sight.

"You sleep okay?" he said.

She was still yawning as Gail walked over to her and handed her a coffee. Mark let his gaze linger as he waited for her to take a swallow and answer him.

"Only had to get up once to go to the bathroom," she said, "but I have to say we can add the spaghetti to the list of meals we'll skip until after the baby is born. Too heavy, and it left me with a lingering heartburn.

Oh, and I got a text from Lisa just now, which is what woke me after I finally settled into a deep sleep, a dream I now can't remember." She pulled her cellphone from the pocket of her housecoat and handed it to him, something he hadn't expected.

"You need to tell her to stop texting so early, or I will," he said.

She only rolled her eyes and walked to the living room, from which he could already feel the heat of the woodstove. "Just read it, Mark, and stop nagging. Important is important."

Mark took a swallow of the steaming coffee and typed in his wife's passcode, then took in the text from Lisa:

Just checked messages at the office about the Palmer kid, Mila. DCFS returned her to her mother last night, but Mom wants to know what happened to her daughter, as she has a red medical incision on her abdomen, left side. I pulled up the file, but nothing shows.

Another text dinged: *Scratch that. Mom is on the warpath. She's at the ER right now. Got a call from the ER doc because Mom has threatened half the staff after they discovered her daughter's left kidney was removed. They want us to go down and take daughter from her. Do I go?*

Mark just stared. He could feel Billy Jo watching him as he squeezed the phone, and he flicked his gaze to her. She lifted her brows, blowing on her mug of steaming coffee, and said nothing. At what point would he need to yank his wife from this cesspool of the DCFS? Stress was stress, and he still couldn't believe she wasn't all over this.

Mark let his gaze linger on Gail and Billy Jo in the living room, his wife now in the leather recliner and Gail adding another piece of wood to the fire. A knock at the door had them both looking his way, and he took in the clock on the stove, which read 7:15 a.m.

"Yeah, I'll get it," was all he said. He put his coffee down beside Billy Jo's phone and strode to the front door, feeling that unease that seemed to build every day and never leave. He flicked the deadbolt, and Lucky was already right beside him, letting out a woof. Sarge quickly followed, barking more.

"Quiet down," Mark said before he pulled open the door and took in two tall men, one in a dark coat, the other a light brown. Something about them screamed Fed, and he spotted the familiar bulge of a sidearm under each of their coats. No badges, but everything about them, the way they stood, the way they stared at him, said enough. He let his gaze linger on their clean-shaven faces and two black SUVs parked behind his Jeep. There were three more men in his driveway, one by the side of the house, wearing dark clothes, and one in military fatigues, watching, standing guard.

What the hell? His heart thudded, and he thought of his gun tucked inside his gun safe in the bedroom. Sloppy. "Can I help you?"

"Are you Mark Friessen?"

He didn't turn around even when he heard footsteps behind him. "Mark, who is it?" Billy Jo said. Damn, why couldn't she stay put? There was the cold fear he recognized and never wanted to feel again.

"Billy Jo, take Lucky and Sarge. Stay in the house." He knew it had come out rather sharply, and he glanced only once to Billy Jo and his baby growing inside her, seeing the moment she understood.

"Come on, you two." She reached for Sarge's collar, then Lucky's, and pulled them back down the hall.

Mark stepped out of the house, barefoot, feeling the chill in the air. He pulled the door closed and wished again that he had his gun. He didn't like being caught off guard. "Who are you, military? Why are you at my house?"

The one at his door, dark hair, close cropped, about Mark's height and build, gestured to him. "Would like to have a word with you," he said. "Wondering if we could talk over here."

He realized it wasn't a question, as the other guy was already down the stairs. Mark took in the security camera outside, which still had to be hooked up, and followed them both down to the side of the house. They walked as if they knew exactly where they were going, and the hair rising at the back of his neck was just another warning about how vulnerable he and his family were. Everything in him was screaming, *What the fuck?*

"Okay, you have me here at the side of my house," he said. "Who the hell are you?" He couldn't make out the other two guys by the vehicle, but he had a feeling they were special forces, maybe. It was just something about the way they stood, the way they were positioned to the side, as if each had a job.

"We're with the military," the dark-haired man said. "We've been following you, Chief Friessen, and we've put together a special unit going after human traffickers, child traffickers. We'd like you to join our team."

He just stared. For a second, he couldn't come up with a reasonable response. "What?" He glanced between the two men. The other was chewing a piece of gum and glancing everywhere but at Mark. He had a mustache, light brown hair, and was a few inches shorter. These men were not desk jockeys, judging by how pumped they appeared, from weights and training or something. "I'm not clear," he said. "You're with the US military?"

"No, not entirely US," said the dark-haired one, jumping in, and Mark picked up something in his accent that said he wasn't from around there.

"Look, boys, I need a little more than what you're giving me," he said. "I'm not entirely comfortable with you showing up at my door, either. My family is here. You say you're not entirely US, so what does that mean, exactly?"

The shorter one with light-brown hair and a mustache dragged his gaze over Mark. His eyes were brown, and the edge in them gave nothing away. "We can't disclose too much," he said. "Let's just say we're a team comprising some former military, some current military, former law enforcement, and former intelligence from the US and a few other countries. What we're doing is putting together a team to put an end to trafficking on a worldwide scale. Right now, I'm sure you're aware human trafficking was once surpassed by guns and drugs, but there's more to it, and we can't say too much unless we get a commitment from you to join our team. We operate under the radar, but we're tackling head-on something that has remained untouchable."

Mark let out a rough laugh, which, he realized, was likely not what they'd expected. He jammed his hands through his thick red hair. He didn't know what to think, and he wondered for a second whether this was a joke.

"I understand you may be a little thrown," the man said. "This is highly unusual, but we're in a different world now, Chief. Let me ask you something. You feel as if your hands are tied at times? We've been following you. We know about the trafficking ring you discovered on the island, the one the old chief was a part of, and the church minister who was a staple of the island. For how many decades have children been moved through here, under the radar? One of your cops was even part of it, and a prominent pediatrician, and how many on the town council were aware? This is only one island. You brought it down single-handedly, but you've found yourself in a constant political battle ever since. You've been looking into every resident of the island because you have a feeling this is bigger than you can imagine. You've battled constant red tape, district attorneys refusing to prosecute, working against you. You're up against a line of predators who can operate unscathed because of who they are and the power they hold. Then there was the social worker before your wife. How many kids disappeared, were trafficked and sold?"

"If I recall," Mark said, knowing he sounded pissed, "you guys showed up and took all the case files, shutting down my investigation into the kids the caseworker was responsible for, who basically disappeared. The missing money and all the evidence is gone."

The dark-haired one had the same expression as the other guy, a hardness that gave nothing away. "Not us," he said.

"It was the military." Mark leaned in, hearing the asshole tone of his voice. He didn't like being blown off.

"Chief, you can't be that naïve," the man said. "You know there are multiple branches within the military.

Units follow the orders they're given and don't even realize that the people whose orders they're following aren't the ones they swore allegiance to. You were over the target, getting too close, and have stepped on toes. Others are watching you, too, not just us."

He thought his ears were ringing. "What? Who's watching me?" He found himself looking over his shoulder. The chill that went up his back bothered him in ways he couldn't have explained to anyone.

"Those whose toes you're stepping on. You don't want to be on their radar. Leaves you with that nice, tingly feeling, doesn't it? Maybe you want to sit with this for a minute. And that camera you have at the front door? You should get it hooked up."

Then both men turned and started walking back to the front.

"Wait," Mark called out. "I don't even know who you are, your names, how to get a hold of you. You just show up here and drop this bomb on me?"

The mustached man looked back to him, and Mark figured he was the one in charge. "You can call me Dion, but understand we didn't have this conversation. We'll give you a bit to think about what we're offering, what it is we're asking of you. Just know that it's best you don't share this with anyone. This isn't a job, Mark Friessen. We're asking you to join the team. There will be training. We're going after these traffickers, after the children. Some we can save, but many we can't. Think about it, Mark. How many children go missing every minute, never to be found again? Who's taking them? This is bigger than you think. We'll give you the morning."

"Wait," Mark said. "I have a wife and a baby on the way."

Dion didn't pull his gaze, which, for the first time, held something that resembled emotion. "Maybe that's another reason we're asking. Again, Mark, we've done our homework on you and your wife, the social worker. Billy Jo, is it?"

He liked this even less, these men he didn't know anything about bringing up his wife. "Who do you work for, then? Who funds you? Who do you report to? I kind of need to know more than what you've told me, just showing up here and asking me to join some task force. I'm the chief on this island. You're asking me to walk away from my job. Who is going to watch over the people here, keep things safe? The former chief wasn't part of it by choice, so you evidently know somebody got to him. My question, are those same somebodies watching me? I won't keep this from my wife. We have no secrets."

Dion gestured to him, standing at the front of the house now. There was no window at that side, and three tall, thick fir trees also sheltered them. They were out of view of everything. "You'll be briefed in full detail when you decide to join the team. You'll sign a military NDA. What you learn will be classified, and you can share only what isn't. You'll have to explain it to your wife. We have our own families, too, who understand that what we're doing is important. You can share the general gist, just not ops. Those details don't get released to anyone outside the team. I shouldn't have to explain why. Your chief was gotten to because the people responsible, who have you in their sight now, operate in the shadows and compromise those they can't buy, those like your former chief, among others."

How much did Mark really know about the intelligence community? Less than he should. For a second, as he stood there, he couldn't get his brain to come up with anything he knew he should be asking. "How do I get a hold of you?"

Dion only shook his head, then started walking, "We'll contact you," he called out over his shoulder.

Mark followed, stepping over the pinecones on the grass, and watched as five men climbed in two SUVs, backed out, and drove away. He took a second, standing in the cool morning air, unable to shake the feeling that he was now at a crossroads, and whatever choice he made would forever change his life.

It was unsettling. His wife was pregnant, but what was the thing he'd always promised her? Kids and animals, he'd sworn to protect them.

L ucky had let out a soft woof as Mark headed out the front door, and he still sat there, waiting, whereas Sarge was already eating his kibble again.

"Lucky, come here, boy. Lie down," Billy Jo said, gesturing sharply to the dog bed in the corner of the living room.

Gail gave the dog a rub as he walked past her and over to his bed, but instead of lying, he sat. "He's just worried," she said. "Doesn't like it when he can't do his job, looking after Mark."

"Yeah, well, the feeling is mutual," Billy Jo said. "You see him out there?"

Gail shook her head, then walked over to the living room to look out the front window. "No, he's out of sight, and that's not a good thing. What do you think they want? Does Mark know them?" She was looking out into the back yard now.

Billy Jo couldn't shake her unease. She knew when Mark was on edge, worried, scared in a way that had him going all alpha like he had a few minutes earlier. It was just a look, his voice, and the tension she could feel coming off him in waves. "I know nothing," Billy Jo said. "That's the problem. I don't know who they are. I don't think Mark does, either, by the way he acted. He just told me to take the dogs."

She heard the door open and put her coffee mug down as she heard Mark's heavy footsteps. He appeared, his gaze intense, tension pulling across those broad shoulders and arms that held her every night.

He said nothing as he walked over to the island, where her phone and his coffee mug were, but instead of reaching for it, he seemed lost in thought.

"Mark, who was that?" she said. "Did you know them? What did they want?"

His hands were now resting on the edge of the island, and he leaned heavily on them before stepping back. How quiet he was in that second really bothered her.

"Mark, what's going on?"

He gave his head a shake. His red hair still had that bedhead look. "I don't know who they are," he said. "Some type of military unit. Special forces, from what I figure. Didn't really say. Didn't offer their names or where they're from, only this cloak and dagger shit. No, I don't know them, but they seem to know all about me."

Mark pushed away from the island, then reached for his mug and took a swallow of his coffee, but it was likely cold, as he walked over to the sink and dumped it out before reaching for the carafe to refill it. Billy Jo glanced over to Gail, who was still standing by the sliding glass door, wearing that motherly look as she watched Mark closely. Then she dragged her gaze to Billy Jo. Okay, so she had picked up on it, as well.

Mark didn't turn around, which had her suspecting that what he said next would be something she wouldn't like. "You remember what happened here, what we found under the minister's house, under the floor?" he said. "The cells, the rooms where he was keeping kids? And the things he was doing with them, selling them? It's something no one wants in their head."

There it was again, that awful knot in her stomach. Mark turned around and let his gaze linger on her, and she could see in his amazing sky-blue eyes that there was way more. She could only nod as she pulled her lower lip between her teeth and instinctually rested her hands on her baby, the flutter of life that she felt throughout the day. Mark's gaze went right to the baby she carried, then over to Gail.

"They offered me a job," he said. "Actually, I don't think it's really a job. It's more that they want me to join a task force or something, considering what I found, that small pedophile ring hidden here. There appear to be many more. I don't even know who those guys are, but if what one of them said is true, they're former cops, military, intelligence…" Mark stopped talking, and she recognized the quiet place he went, seeming to hold on to things. He stared into his mug of coffee and then shook his head, making a face. "When I first became a deputy, I never expected to find what I did on this island. I've had my eyes opened in ways I never thought possible. I believed the world to be one way, but I'm starting to think everything I thought to be true was a lie. I knew deep down that the problem wasn't isolated to this island." He let his gaze linger, and she had an awful feeling of an impending change.

"So what does this mean, exactly, Mark?" she said. She knew Gail hadn't moved, just listening to everything. "You have a job as the chief on this island. This is our home."

Mark's face told her everything he hadn't said, and it really hit home. "I think you know what it means. From the little they said, if I join this team, I won't be chief here anymore. That's all I know. It's military, but not what we think of. I don't know all the details. Seems they operate under the radar, which is the only way to go after the kind of corruption we're talking about. Drugs and illegal guns have been coming across our border, out of control, for so long, but human trafficking has exceeded everything. You know what I'm talking about—kids, babies, women. This is about taking them down, and that's all I know. I'll know the details only if I decide to join. Some things are classified, and no one outside the team can know. I think you already know that the people involved in trafficking are in positions of power. They have access to everything, and they have people everywhere."

Billy Jo put down her mug of coffee. "And why does it have to be you?"

He walked over to her after setting his own mug down and rested his hands on her shoulders, then ran them down over her arms so tenderly, lovingly. "I didn't say yes," he said. "They want me to think about it. Only if I commit to joining them will I know more. I'm not taking on something without talking to you. I'm telling you what I know and what they want. For all I know, this could be someone messing with me."

"I don't think you believe that, Mark," Gail cut in.

Billy Jo turned to her. Gail's expression was tense and heavy, and from the face she made, Billy Jo wondered whether she was thinking again of what Tolly had done. She didn't know how she'd feel if it had been Mark.

"We've never talked about what happened," Gail said, "not really. But think about it. Who has that kind of power, to have gotten to my husband through my son, having him agreeing to look the other way as innocent kids were preyed on? It wouldn't just be here. How many others are involved? How deep does this go, how far up the chain of command? The low-hanging fruit, the working class, is doing the dirty work, but how many are pulling the strings, controlling this? They have the power and money to control the system, so who has that kind of power?"

Billy Jo felt Mark squeeze her arm as if he needed to hold on to it.

"I think you and I both know we're talking at a level above governments," he said. "But, as I said, I haven't accepted anything, and I may not even hear from them again. Speaking of which, about that text from Lisa, I'll call her and handle it. I'm going to grab a shower and head in to work." He pressed a kiss to her forehead. "Why don't you stay home this morning, put your feet up and take it easy?" He let his fingers run gently down the side of her face.

"No, I'm right behind you," she said. "I have some files I need to clean up, calls to make, and I plan to be there when you have your chit-chat with Lisa. One thing I've learned about her is that she loves to go down the rabbit hole, finding things and digging in places the average person will never go, but it could be just another screwup."

He said nothing. For a second, she wondered whether he'd tell her no, but he just nodded and lingered there, and she pressed the flat of her hand to his chest. It was so instinctual to touch him. Then he was walking away, into the bedroom, and Billy Jo turned to Gail, who was shaking her head.

"Who do you think those men work for?" Billy Jo said. "The military? What do you think he meant about a task force? Who's overseeing it, funding it? I really don't like this." She pressed her hand to her own chest.

Gail made another face and looked down at her coffee. "You know what, Billy Jo? Mark's right about one thing: You should put your feet up and take it easy this morning." She walked over to the coffeepot and refilled her mug. "I think I'm going to grab a quick shower, too."

Then Gail walked away and down the stairs, and Billy Jo realized that for all the questions she had, Gail likely had more. But she would tread only so far down that road back to the horror that had her living with them.

Billy Jo listened to the water running, her husband still in the shower. Mark was holding back something. Whatever it was, she'd do her own digging and find out who had shown up on her doorstep and what kind of team, exactly, they wanted her husband to join.

Mark sat in his idling Jeep as he pulled up Lisa's number and dialed. He slipped his cell phone in the dash mount before shifting the vehicle into reverse and backing out of the driveway. The trail of smoke rose from the chimney ahead, and he glanced into the empty back seat, missing Lucky, who had once gone everywhere with him. Then they had inherited Sarge, the light lab, and these days, knowing both dogs were always with Billy Jo let him breathe a little easier.

"This is Lisa."

"Lisa, this is Chief Friessen," Mark said. "You sent my wife a text this morning about a problem with a kid who was returned to her mother. I understand she's at the hospital and there may be some trouble." He took in the falling leaves as he turned onto the main road into town.

"Right, okay." She hesitated. "When Billy Jo didn't answer, I kind of made a judgement call."

He wondered how often his wife still wanted to

wring Lisa's neck. "Billy Jo was sleeping," he said. "You woke her up with your text, and she read it and gave it to me. So now I want to know what's going on—and what, exactly, do you mean by a judgement call?"

The sky was gray, but there was no rain. The wind was picking up here and there, and the trees rustled, the leaves blowing in a few spots across the gravel road.

"Well, I'm at the ER," Lisa said, "actually just pulling in, and I plan on having a word with Mila's mom and the doctor who called. I suspect a clerical error in the file, but I'm sure there's a logical explanation. With her showing up and going ballistic…"

Mark shook his head, knowing nothing was that simple. "You know what? Don't go in. Just wait outside until I get there. I'm only a few minutes away." Instead of driving straight into town, he turned left at the hospital.

"Okay," Lisa said. "Chief, this really could be just a matter of someone forgetting to make a note in the file, or a report is still sitting on the desk of whoever updates everything online, or it could be lost or passed to a supervisor who misfiled it or added it to one of many piles." She could go on and on sometimes.

He took in the parking lot to the hospital as he pulled in. "I get it," he said, "but now I'm here. I'll meet you out front." He pressed the end icon as he found a spot in one of the four rows and pulled in. For an island hospital, it was busier than expected.

Mark stepped out of his Jeep and closed the door. Walking to the front, wearing his jean jacket, he felt the familiar weight of his sidearm fastened to his jeans, and he couldn't have put into words how naked he felt without it. He spotted Lisa walking toward him from a row over, wearing dark-rimmed glasses, blue jeans, and a gray coat that went to her knees, her dark hair back in a ponytail. He noted the blue compact she'd just climbed out of.

"Hi, Chief," she said. "So is Billy Jo coming, as well? I didn't hear back from her and was going to send another text to let her know where I am."

Mark only shook his head as Lisa fell in beside him. She was short, in flat boots. He gave her a passing glance as he took in the door to the emergency room. A man outside, in a blue coat, was smoking a cigarette. "No, she's at home," he said. "I'm handling this, so fill me in on everything that happened."

The doors slid open. Behind the security desk was a man in a white shirt, black pants, and a badge, with a walkie talkie at his side. In the waiting room to his left were about five people.

Lisa headed for the window of the nurses' station and tapped on it. "Mila Palmer was returned to her mother, Irene Palmer," she began, then leaned on the counter as the window slid open.

A nurse was behind the plexiglass. "Just wait your turn," she said.

"I'm Lisa Jenkins, with the DCFS. I was called about Mila Palmer. This is Chief Friessen." She was holding up her ID, and the nurse was already nodding. Then there was a buzz—the door to the ER, which was apparently kept locked.

"Come on in," was all the nurse said before she rose and pushed open the door. She had short dark hair and was older, with at least four inches on Lisa. "That girl's mama is carrying on. I'll take you back to Doctor Collins."

Mark held the door as Lisa walked through, and he took in the busy ER, with curtained-off areas, the phone ringing, people on gurneys. A security guard was standing at the last curtained-off area, where the nurse was leading them.

"I was checking messages early this morning," Lisa told him, continuing, "and Irene Palmer called sometime last night after discovering an incision on her daughter's abdomen. She said it was still red, as if stitches had been removed. She's demanding to know what happened. I checked the file online, and there's nothing about a medical emergency or surgery. The ER doc on call here said she showed up, issuing threats to half the staff."

Mark glanced away from her to see that a short man with neat dark hair was walking their way, in blue scrubs.

"Doctor Collins, this is the social worker and the chief of police about the Palmer woman," the nurse said, gesturing to Mark and Lisa.

"Marshall Collins," he said. "I'm the ER doctor on call right now." He held his hand out to Mark. He was maybe five foot three, not much taller than Lisa and a lot shorter than Mark, but he appeared to work out, with an ultra-conservative clean-cut vibe.

"Chief Friessen," Mark said, "and this is Lisa Jenkins, from the DCFS." He shook the man's hand, and so did Lisa. "You want to fill me in on what's going on? Where are the Palmers, the mom and daughter?"

The ER doctor gestured to the corner. "Over here," he said. "I called security when she tried to leave. I have to tell you, Chief, she's evidently unhinged. She came in here and threatened the staff, pounded on the glass at the front, and was hostile to the nurses, yelling and screaming expletives. She refused to hear reason, instead rambling off accusations and demands about what happened to her daughter, saying we did something to her. I'm recommending she be held until a psychiatric assessment can be carried out. I called family services to take Mila."

Mark could see the security guard, but the doctor was standing in front of them, his arms crossed, glancing from him to Lisa and back. He was soft spoken.

"Mila was just returned to her mom yesterday," Lisa said. "She left a message at the office saying there was a surgical incision on her daughter. Is that true?"

Mark watched as the doctor shook his head and made a face, then said, "I haven't even looked at her. Her mom was too irate. When I asked to have a look, she started in on me, so that was when I called family services. This is upsetting Mila, and the mother can't be reasoned with."

"Now that we're here, let's go have a talk with the Palmers," Mark said. "I know I want to hear what she has to say." He gestured behind the doctor, who, for a second, appeared confused. Maybe he'd just expected them to take Mila. However, the doctor soon led them to the curtained-off area, and as he fell in beside him, Mark said, "So how does this psych assessment happen? Do you just decide to lock her up?"

"It's based on my recommendation, and yes, security and staff from Psychiatry will come down and get her. She'll be put on a forty-eight-hour hold, and then the head of psychiatry will decide further. Thanks, Jerry," he said to the security guard. "This is the social worker and Chief Friessen. She say anything to you?"

Mark took in the doctor, unable to shake the impression of arrogance.

"Some nasty four-letter words," the guard said. "Tried to leave, but I told her to knock it off or it would go worse for her." He stepped aside.

Mark said nothing, only brushed the curtain open to see a woman with dark hair, shoulder length, a mass of messy waves, sitting in a chair by the foot of the bed. Her face was round, her brown eyes wide, and she was holding a little girl who wore a red coat, sneakers, and blue pants.

"Hi, are you Irene?" he said. "And you must be Mila. I'm Chief Friessen. I understand you got your daughter back last night and there was a problem?" He knew Lisa was right behind him by the way Irene's eyes tracked her and the doctor, who had also walked in and was standing at the other side of the bed.

"I'm not talking to him," Irene said, tilting her head to the doctor, who had set his hands on the bed. "He's trying to take my daughter from me."

"No, you're talking to me," Mark said. He gestured to the doctor with his thumb. "Don't look at him; look at me. This is just you and me talking. Can you tell me what happened?"

He didn't miss how tightly she held her daughter. The little girl, whose hood was down, was clutching her mother's brown sweater coat, and her eyes, the same brown, held a fear he didn't like seeing in a child.

"Hey there, Mila," he said. "I'm not going to hurt you. I'm Chief Friessen, but you can call me Mark." He let his gaze linger on the little girl as she turned her head back to her mother, holding on tight.

"Tell you what happened?" Irene said. "I've been

fighting these people for two years to get my daughter back, being denied visitation, then being allowed supervised visits only. Last night, I was bathing her and saw a scar, a long one, on her left side. It's still fresh and red. I know a surgical scar. I'm not an idiot. I want to know what you did to my daughter!"

Mark made himself pull in a breath, feeling the accusation and anger in the bite of her words. This mother was out for blood. "Can I see?" he said. "I'm here to help, and I hear your anger. I get it, but let's first get to the bottom of what happened."

She didn't pull her gaze from him. From how rough her breathing was, he knew she was likely terrified of the corner she'd been backed into. Then she looked down to her daughter and said, "Mila, sit up. Come on." She helped her daughter sit and turn. Her coat was unzipped, and she wore a faded pink shirt, which Irene lifted. The incision line, still red, went around her side.

Mark stepped back and glanced over to the doctor. "Have you seen this? What is that from?" He gestured to the girl, then shoved his hand in his pocket. Lisa was staring, narrowing her eyes.

"You're not laying a hand on my daughter," Irene snapped, as Doctor Collins had taken a step around the gurney and stopped just beside Mark.

"Irene, look at me," Mark said. "I'm not leaving, and I promise you Doctor Collins is just going to take a look so we can get to the bottom of this. That's all." He forced calmness into his voice.

Irene considered what he'd said, still holding her daughter tight, then nodded and looked up at Mark. "He's not giving her anything or taking her anywhere."

Mark shook his head. "You have my word, Irene. I'm staying here. The doctor is just looking."

Marshall Collins squatted down in front of Irene and lifted his hands. "I'm just going to touch it," he said to the little girl, who was now standing between her mother's legs. "Does that hurt?"

Mila looked to her mother. He wondered, by the way she flinched, if the scar was tender still. "It's sore," she said to her mom.

The doctor stood up and turned to Mark, rubbing his hand over his chin, his back to Irene. "Can I have a word with you, Chief?" was all he said.

Mark glanced back to Lisa and then over to the distrust staring back at him from Irene. "Okay, Irene, I'll be right back," he said before pushing aside the curtain and stepping out. Lisa followed.

They followed the doctor a few steps before he turned, one arm pulled over his chest, the other hand on his chin. His expression only added to Mark's unease.

"Well?" Mark said.

"That's an incision to remove a kidney," Doctor Collins said in a low voice.

Mark glanced over to Lisa, who, for the first time ever, was quiet. "You know anything about this?"

She shook her head. "No, there was nothing in the file I pulled up."

Mark looked back to the doctor, who had walked over to a long desk with a computer and was typing something in.

"Mila Palmer? There's nothing on her at this hospital." Doctor Collins looked over to him.

Lisa stepped forward, right up to the desk. "Mila

was in foster care off island," she said. "She was moved a couple times, but her last placement was in Seattle."

Mark stared. He'd never understood everything about how the system worked. "That's a ways. How often does that happen?" Maybe he needed to sit down and have Billy Jo brief him on why kids were sent so far from home.

"It happens in special cases, special needs," Lisa said. "I'm not really sure."

The doctor was typing again.

"Ah, there you are. So what did you find out?"

Mark turned to see his pregnant wife, wearing a long brown sweater, her new large fall coat, and blue jeans. "Hey," he said. "I thought you were going to stay home and take it easy this morning?"

She slid her hand in his as he leaned down and kissed her, linking his fingers with hers. She shrugged. "No, I made a couple calls and knew you were both here. So what did I miss?"

"Okay, well, this is interesting," Doctor Collins cut in.

Mark dragged his gaze back to the doctor, who stared at the screen. "What is?"

"You said Seattle. I interned at the children's hospital in Seattle, and there's a discharge record for a Mila Palmer after a kidney removal. Healthy kidney, from the report here, for donation." The doctor only shook his head, his expression grim.

"Excuse me, did you say a donation?" Mark said.

The doctor made a face, still staring at the screen. "From what I can see."

Mark glanced back to his wife, who was staring up at

him, watchful, and then over to Lisa, who opened her mouth to say something but pulled in a breath instead.

"Let me get this straight," Mark said. "That little girl in there donated a kidney while in the care of the state?"

No one said anything.

"The mother doesn't know." Mark found himself looking over to the curtained-off area and the security guard who still lingered close by. "Well, as I see it, this is a problem. Who authorized this?" He looked back to his wife, who gripped his hand. Lisa had looked over to Billy Jo for answers, and the doctor said nothing.

"Come on, someone needs to give me some answers here," Mark said. "Irene over there is out for blood, and as I see it, she's got every right to demand answers and to be pissed."

Billy Jo pulled her hand from his and ran it over his arm, holding on to him. "Before anything else, someone needs to tell Irene."

He pictured the mother who had fought to get her daughter back. "You want me to do it?"

Billy Jo made a face. "No, I think I'd better. Maybe you can do what you do best and find out who authorized the removal of her kidney. Who did it, and why, and who was it given to? Find that out, because a four-year-old girl isn't old enough to decide, let alone understand what she's given up."

Damn, he knew she was right, but he needed a minute to wrap his head around this shitshow. He turned back to the doctor, who was still behind the computer, as his wife and Lisa started back to the curtain-off area where the Palmers were.

"Okay, Doc," Mark said. "You pull up everything in there for me. I want the doctor's name and all the medical staff who took that little girl's kidney. Who signed for it? I need everything in the records, because someone is going to answer for this."

The doctor stepped back and pulled his arms over his chest. "I'll see what I can dig up, but I'm going to need to examine the girl, as that incision is still fresh. Then there's the issue with the mother. I've already ordered a psych hold on her."

Mark stared at the ER doctor and let out a rough laugh under his breath that should have been a warning. "Are you fucking kidding me?" he bit out, then gestured sharply to the curtained-off area. "That little girl's kidney was taken out, no one bothered to tell the mother, and you're still pushing this?"

"She threatened the nurses and me. She was yelling, out of control, and couldn't be reasoned with."

"And you don't think she had a reason to be?"

The doctor only pulled in a breath. "I agree this is troublesome, but this is for the safety of the child."

Mark just stared at him. He knew that unless he convinced the doctor to see reason, the only avenue Irene had was to find a sympathetic judge who could and would override him.

CHAPTER
Four

"Hi, Irene," Billy Jo said. "I'm Billy Jo McCabe. My husband is Chief Mark Friessen." She rested her hand on her baby, a protective instinct that had come from nowhere one day.

The woman staring up at her, who had been just a name in a file, had a spooked look. Her brown coat, faux fur, was fraying at the wrists, and she held her little girl tightly in her arms. Mila was resting her head against her mother's chest.

"He said he would be right back," Irene said, "though I'm not sure I believe him. So why'd he send you in? I'm not letting you take her again." She was looking right at Lisa now.

Billy Jo shot her a sharp glance when she heard her pull in a breath, about to say something, and quickly said, "No one is taking anyone right now," as much to Lisa as to Irene, who had flinched back the fear she was trying to hide.

Irene lowered her gaze, taking in Billy Jo's pregnant

belly. "You and the chief are having a baby, so you understand," she said. "Are you a cop, too?"

What was she supposed to say to that?

"No, I'm not a cop. I'm a social worker here—actually, the managing social worker on the island. I understand that you as a mother want answers, and I don't know how I'd feel if I saw what you did. The doctor said the incision would have been to remove a kidney."

Irene's expression was one of horror. She seemed to hold her daughter tighter, and tears filled her eyes. "What? Her kidney, what are you talking about? Her kidney was taken out? How is that possible?"

Billy Jo squatted in front of her and touched Irene's hand, the one that held her daughter. She reached for the foot of the hospital bed so she wouldn't fall over. "I am so sorry," she started, but Irene ripped her hand away as if she couldn't stand her touch, and now the look staring back at her was filled with hatred.

"You're sorry!" she cried. "You took my baby away because a damn doctor told you to. Two years ago, I came into this emergency room because my girl was sick with a bad cough, congested. I expected something when they ran tests, but they found nothing, yet the doctor wanted to pump her full of powerful antibiotics for a few days, give her a bunch of drugs, hook her up to an IV because he thought it might help even though he said he didn't know what the problem was. Then he said he also wanted to do a spinal tap. I said no, he wasn't guessing on my daughter and pumping her full of drugs when he didn't know what was wrong with her. I said no because I realized I was dealing with someone who wasn't focused on figuring out the problem, just going right to heavy drugs. So I said I was taking her home so

I could get a second opinion from a different doctor. You know what happened next? Two years of me fighting the damn system that stole my baby from me. I've got nothing, I'm broke, and now you've taken her kidney?"

Billy Jo heard the curtain brush back and felt a hand on her arm as she struggled to stand. Mark was right there, looking down at her as he helped her up. He was so strong. She didn't know how to tell Irene that it hadn't been her. It had been before she arrived on the island.

"Irene, the doctor is going to come in," Mark said. "He has an ultrasound just to take a look."

Irene was shaking her head. Billy Jo recognized a woman ready to run out the door, and could she blame her? No.

Mark was standing in front of her. "I get that you're pissed," he said, "and you have every right to be, but do not yell at my wife. She didn't take your daughter. She's only trying to help. Let the doctor have a look. No one seems to know what's going on, but I'm damn sure going to find out. It's just an ultrasound, Irene."

Billy Jo didn't know how he did that. Behind her, a woman in blue scrubs with a brown sweater pulled overtop wheeled in an ultrasound machine. Lisa moved aside, and the doctor was there now too, making the small space overcrowded. Mark somehow had Irene moving Mila onto the bed. Billy Jo had to look up, her eyes burning. Damn, he was going to be such a great father.

"You okay, babe?" Mark said to her. He was right there, his hand on her arm. The last thing she wanted was to cry in the middle of this shitshow. Maybe he knew, as he shielded her as she wiped a hand under her eye when a tear fell.

"Yeah, just being pregnant," she said. She wondered if he knew that was bullshit. He let his gaze linger, his hand on her, always touching her. She reached out and pressed the flat of her hand to his chest, and then he leaned in and pressed a kiss to her forehead, holding her for just a second.

"Well, it's as I thought," the doctor said. "Right here, her left kidney was taken out. I'd guess by the looks of the incision that it happened two to three weeks ago. I'd like to run some tests."

Mark was standing beside Billy Jo, and she had her hand on his arm, over the heavy jean jacket.

"You're not putting another hand on my daughter or running any more tests," Irene said. "I want to know why this happened. I should have been told if she was sick."

"You should have been told a lot of things, Irene," Billy Jo said, taking in the little girl on the hospital bed. She appeared so scared, and her mother was holding her hand. "Lisa, was there anything in the file to give you an idea of the reason for this?"

Lisa was unusually quiet. "Found nothing when I pulled it up online, but as I said to the chief, the information could be in a form or memo not filed or updated online. I don't think the original file has come back yet. I can do some digging."

"Go do that."

Lisa hesitated only a second. "Okay, you mean now? What about Mila?"

Billy Jo realized Irene was holding her daughter again, standing at the other side of the gurney. "I'm here," she said. "I'll handle this. You go and start digging."

As Lisa brushed back the curtain and stepped out, Billy Jo let her hand fall away from Mark. She caught a glimpse of the security guard and what looked like two orderlies just outside the curtain as if waiting, and she knew it was about the Palmers.

"Doctor Collins, what kinds of tests are you wanting to run?" she said. She took in the mom and realized everything was going to be a fight.

"Well, Mila had a kidney removed, and even though she's young, recovery for that operation is long. But being a living donor also carries all kinds of complications. She has only one kidney now, which means it has to increase in size to compensate for the loss, and that comes with problems. Mainly, she needs to have a blood and urine test for her kidney function and blood pressure, because she now has a greater risk of problems, one being reduced kidney function. We need to monitor her closely."

The ultrasound was being packed up, and the technician, with her hair pinned back, was pushing it back out. One of the orderlies, both in off-white scrubs, held the curtain open for her and said, "Dr. Collins, we're ready to bring her up." At the look passing between him and the doctor, Billy Jo's heart thudded. The two orderlies walked around her.

"Dr. Collins, what is this?" she said. "Mark, what's going on?"

Mark's expression was grim, and he had his arm around her, moving her out of the curtained-off area. Behind her, Irene was screaming, swearing, yelling, and Mila gave a cry as she was ripped from her mother. Another orderly came running over with a gurney.

"Mark, what is this?"

"The ER doctor ordered Irene held for a psych evaluation," he said. "I can't do anything. My hands are tied on this, Billy Jo. She came in here on fire, shouting threats, angry, though I can't blame her." He gestured back with both hands, and she sensed his frustration. She listened to Mila crying and watched as Irene, now on a gurney, quiet and apparently sedated, was wheeled out.

"I have no power here," Mark said. "Damn, I never paid any attention to how doctors can just do this. You have any ideas? If you do, I'm all ears. I tried to talk the doctor down, and I thought I got him to see reason, but evidently, he had his mind made up and had already set the ball in motion." He scratched his head. His red hair was wavy, kept shorter now than it once had been.

"How long is the psych hold?" she said.

Mark was pacing back and forth in front of her. There were times he carried everything. He gestured in the air. "Forty-eight hours is what he said."

Billy Jo pressed her lips together, hearing whimpers from Mila, who'd already been taken from her mother for so long. "She'll get a hearing at some point. Only problem, Mark, is that now Mila is back in the system, and judges always lean toward the recommendations of doctors and social workers," she said. *If only it were that simple,* she thought.

"Not necessarily," he said. "Judges are wild cards; you don't know what they're going to do."

"This needs to be flagged," Billy Jo said. "I'll put in my recommendation and fight the fight for her, but Irene needs a good lawyer. Like most kids in the system, Mila lives in poverty, and her mom not having anything is what will keep her in it."

Maybe Mark understood her frustration, as he reached over and ran his hand over her shoulder. "So will this be another two years that her daughter will be taken from her?" he said. "Was it really the fact that she wanted a second opinion from a different doctor that caused her to lose her kid? I can't believe this. That four-year-old girl has had her kidney taken out and you don't even know why? That is some pretty serious, under-handed, fucked-up shit."

What could she say to Mark? Billy Jo had counted it as a win the day before when she'd heard Mila had been returned to her mother on the island. "All I know, Mark, from my brief read of the file, is that a doctor called the social worker who was here before me, Link Stone, and his notes in the file said Mila was really sick. According to him, the tests came back showing nothing, so he wanted to run a heavy round of antibiotics to be on the safe side and then do a spinal tap. Mom said that sounded a little extreme, and she wasn't keen on heavy antibiotics being pumped into a little girl, so the doctor made the call to Link, saying Irene was denying medical care to her daughter.

"There's nothing in the file to suggest she was going for a second opinion. The notes said only that there was possible neglect and the mom was refusing care. The doctor stalled her with paperwork until Link got there, even put a security guard by the door until Link could take custody of Mila. Two years later and many hearings, and Irene couldn't afford a lawyer, so the judge relied solely on the doctor's opinion and the testimony of the social worker, who was Link. But Irene didn't give up. I know Mila's last home was in Seattle." She had so many questions. She couldn't hear Mila crying anymore.

"What do you want to do?" she asked, realizing she depended on Mark so much.

"I'm going to find out what happened to that little girl's kidney," he said. "Maybe you can find out which social worker in Seattle made the decision, see if there are any clerical errors like Lisa said. A four-year-old in foster care donating a kidney? Sorry, but something smells here. I'm going to head in to the station. You want to walk out with me?"

The curtain had been brushed back. Billy Jo ran her hand over his arm and shook her head. "No, you go. I need to take care of some things here with Mila. I'll call you later?"

Mark leaned in and kissed her. "Call me if there's a problem," he said. Then he walked away, her husband, a man she loved more than she had words to describe.

She spotted the ER doctor as he walked back around the counter, and all she could think was that she was glad she'd decided to have her baby at home with a midwife. The only problem was that she hadn't yet told Mark.

Mark pulled up in front of the police station to see a black SUV parked in his spot. Lacy's tracker and Carmen's cruiser were off to the side. His anxiety built at what felt like another thing coming out of left field. As soon as he walked through the door, both Lacy and Carmen stared his way from where they stood at Lacy's desk. His gaze went right to his office, where Dion and another man he'd never seen before waited.

"Mark," was all Lacy got out as he closed the door.

"Yeah, I see," he said. "Listen, I just left the hospital. Carmen, I want you to follow up with Lisa Jenkins. She's looking into a little girl, Mila Palmer, who was just returned to her mother from foster care yesterday. The problem is that she was returned without one of her kidneys. The incision is fresh."

He didn't know who appeared more shocked, Lacy or Carmen.

"This is a joke, right?" Lacy said.

Mark was already shaking his head. "Nope, afraid

not. Billy Jo is still at the hospital. Give her a call there. I think she's sorting out things for the little girl. Long story, but the mom showed up there furious and lost it, threatening the staff, among other things, because she'd discovered the incision in her daughter's side. The ER doc has ordered the mother, Irene, be held over for a psych evaluation because of how she went off. Nothing I can do there, but I want to know the who, what, and where of how a four-year-old in the care of the state donated a kidney. It was done at Seattle Children's. Find out everyone involved, who signed off on it, who took her there, and what doctors, nurses, and orderlies were involved in the decision. And I mean everyone. Do not leave a stone unturned."

"Mark," Lacy said again, gesturing behind him. Mark turned to see Dion standing in his doorway, in blue jeans, his stance all military.

"Chief, if you have a moment," he said, gesturing into the office.

Mark realized it wasn't a request. "I'll be right there," he snapped, feeling the weight of everything. Then he turned back to Lacy, not missing the empty dog bed, knowing both were at home with Gail. "Lacy, hold my calls…"

"I know, Chief, unless it's Billy Jo," she cut in, evidently knowing his wife came first.

Mark turned to take in the two men who'd invaded his small office, both standing as he strode in and closed the door. He stepped around Dion and then his desk, shrugging out of his jean jacket and tossing it over the hook on his coat tree.

He took his time before turning to the men. "Well, I didn't expect this," he said.

The other man, the one he didn't remember from that morning, was older, his hair wavy and shoulder length, a mix of light and gray—not exactly military protocol, he thought. "We gave you time to consider our offer."

Mark realized they were serious. "I expected a little more than a couple hours. I'm kind of in the middle of something, and who the fuck are you?" He realized it had come out quite sharply. He let his gaze land on the guy, who appeared more like a bum than a military man. He was getting a feeling he didn't like.

The man, though, he realized, didn't seem bothered in the least. He suspected he had to be around ten years older than he was, in a faded t-shirt with a leather jacket overtop and worn blue jeans. "We heard about that 'something,'" he said, then held his hand over Mark's desk between them. "Mike Smith."

Mark stared at his hand and hesitated only a second before he shook it. It was rough, strong. Mike's eyes were a deeper blue than his, and it appeared as if he hadn't shaved in a week.

"You were saying something out there about a little girl missing a kidney," Mike said. "She was in foster care. How old?"

"Four." He didn't know why he'd answered.

"Let me guess: There's no record. Even though she was in the care of the state, and it happened at a children's hospital, the records that should be there are missing."

That constant knot in his stomach was back. "How would you know that?" he said, and the exchange between the two men bothered him more than anything.

"What did I say to you this morning about the trafficking of kids, babies, women?" Mike said. "You know why they're trafficked and for what? Organs are only a small part of it. The kids are used in ways that would leave you without a peaceful night's sleep ever again. Not many can do this work, Mark. It takes something out of us, what we see, the horrors no one would believe are committed by people who are untouchable.

"There are a lot of really bad people in this world. I'm sure you think it's about cutting off the head of the snake, but once you do, a hundred more are waiting to take its place. Think about what it takes to run the world, because basically, this is what we're talking about. The world is not what you were taught in school. Who do you think created the systems schools teach you to believe in?

"You have one case of a little girl whose kidney was taken. Let me tell you how it will shake out: You'll spend weeks on it, getting names, and some low-level social worker or government bureaucrat will take the fall. It'll be blamed on paperwork, a clerical error. Dummy records will be produced. You'll get a lot of 'Oops, sorry, we don't know how it happened,' but the scapegoat will be fired or shuffled off to another state, maybe given a nice bonus to shut their fucking mouth. NDAs will be signed so no one talks.

"And even if you try to pursue something, what it comes down to is that the state assumes all medical care for foster children and the right to make all medical decisions because that's the law. Even though her kidney is gone, you won't be able to go after anyone. It will be buried. There will be no news report, because even if you find a journalist who has the balls to investigate and write a story, it will never go to print because it won't get past the gatekeeper's desk. Your hands will be tied everywhere you turn."

Mark pulled his arms across his chest, wanting to swear under his breath. This Mike Smith had just summed up what was very likely going to happen. "How do you know all this?"

"What's the girl's name?"

"Mila Palmer."

Dion had his phone out already, texting something, but by the dynamics, it seemed as if Mike was in charge. "We'll have someone look into it, but she's one of too many. Organs, especially from babies and young children, are sought after. It's noble, the way you're looking even though you can't do anything. We're going to need your answer."

"And I'm going to need a little more from you," Mark said, knowing he still sounded like an asshole. "I'm the chief on this island, and I can't just quit. Then they'll bring in someone else who'll turn a blind eye when paid enough to look the other way."

"Look, Chief, we're not here to twist your arm. We just need a yes or no. But maybe you should ask yourself about that little girl this morning. You won't be able to do anything about her by playing whack-a-mole and not making a dent. We're not going in and saving as many of these souls as we can; we're taking down organizations from the middle all the way up. The son of former chief Tolly Shephard was kidnapped and tortured, among other things, to force his father into compliance. Yes, we know. We'll leave you now, but here's my number. It will be in service only until eight tonight. That's all the time you have." Mike Smith held out a piece of paper with a number on it.

Mark reached for it and took in both men. "I need more from you both on the where, the how, the details. I have a wife and a baby on the way."

Mike tilted his head to the door, and Dion pulled it open and stepped out before pulling it closed behind him. "I can tell you this: You'll be flown to our training base and meet the team. You'll sign a nondisclosure and be given classified information on operations in key locations based on tips provided by a wide network, let's just say. You heard about the massive cargo ship grounded just off the shore of Vancouver with those containers six months ago?"

Mark cleared his throat. "Sure, vaguely."

Mike didn't smile. "That was us. You know what we found?"

There it was, that sick feeling again. "Sure, guns, drugs…"

Mike's expression gave nothing away. "Guns and drugs, sure, always a given. But of the eighteen thousand containers, do you want to know about the kids we found alive? And the ones who weren't? Not everyone can handle the horrors these people are capable of. This takes its toll on everyone, Mark, and not everyone can do it. This is bigger than you and me.

"We'd like you to join us. Talk to your wife. But if I can leave you with one thing, it's that yes, you have a wife and a baby on the way, but these people we're up against know everything about you now—what you eat for breakfast, the stray dog you named Lucky and the lab called Sarge that you took in when his owner mysteriously died or disappeared. They know your weakness for animals and how to get to you. As long as they're out there, operating in the shadows, your wife and your unborn child will never be safe. If they got to Tolly Shepherd after what they did to his son, what do you think they would do to a baby to get your compliance?"

Mike rested his hand on the door and pulled it open, then looked back just a second before stepping out.

Mark stared at the number in his hand, hearing the outside door close as the two men left. The phone was ringing, and Lacy answered. He walked over to his office door and closed it, shutting his eyes for a second. If anyone ever laid a hand on Billy Jo or his baby, he knew with certainty he'd kill that person.

He made himself pull in a breath and yanked his door open to see Carmen at her desk as she hung up her phone, too. "Carmen, you have the number for that home security company you referred me to?"

"You mean the one that installed the camera at your house?" She pulled open her desk drawer.

"No, the monitoring company to hook it up and put it online."

She pulled a card from her drawer and walked it over to Mark. "You said it was too expensive," she said, and he saw the question in her eyes as he took the business card. He knew the company was one of the best.

"I changed my mind. Thanks," he said. Then, just as Lacy hung up the phone, he called out, "Lacy, call this security company and get them to hook up the system at my house, the cameras, the alarm, everything." He handed the card to Lacy and then strode back to his office and reached for his jean jacket.

"Sure," she said, standing in the doorway, having followed him. "Do you have a day in mind to schedule with them?"

Mark couldn't shake his unease. "Now. Tell them I

want it hooked up and running before the day is out." He pulled his keys from his pocket and took in Lacy and Carmen's wide-eyed expressions, then pulled his cell phone from his pocket and dialed Billy Jo's number. It rang only once.

"I'm just leaving the hospital," she said. "Did you find out anything?"

"Can you meet me at home?" He turned away from the door, knowing Lacy and Carmen were listening.

"Well, I have to go in to the office. I want to talk to Lisa, and…"

"This is important, Billy Jo."

She hesitated. "Okay. Is everything okay?"

What the hell was he supposed to say to the woman he loved? "Everything is fine. I just need to talk to you, and it can't be over the phone."

"I'm on my way," she said, then hung up, and Mark shoved his phone in his pocket and started around his desk. In the bullpen, both women were staring at him as if they'd figured out something was wrong.

"Lacy, I need you to call now," he said. "Carmen, handle things here until I get back." He walked to the door and pulled it open.

"Chief, what did those men want?" Carmen said.

Mark shook his head. "Nothing I can talk about right now," he said. Then he stepped out of the sheriff's office and pulled the door closed.

For a moment, he just stood there on the sidewalk, taking in the people across the road, the cars driving by, the shops up the street, and the familiar hotel and restaurant across the road, trying to get a sense of anyone or anything that seemed out of place.

Billy Jo spotted Mark in his Jeep behind her as she pulled into their driveway and parked beside Gail's pickup. By the time she had turned off her car and reached for her bag, Mark was already opening her door and holding out his hand.

"You know I can still get out," she said.

The hint of a smile pulled at his lips. "I know, but humor me, considering you're the one who has to carry the baby."

She settled her hand in his and stepped out, and his hand slid over her back as she slipped her bag over her shoulder. Mark closed her door.

"How did everything go at the hospital?" he said.

What was she supposed to say? Her job now was to make sure Mila had a home, a bed, a place to go. She knew she could fight only so much of the system before the little girl became a file on someone else's desk. "Mila has been admitted to the hospital for follow-up care. Irene is locked in the psych ward under a forty-eight-hour hold, which means no one can see or talk to her. I tried to reach the psychiatrist who runs the department. Had to become a pain in the ass for the nurse and intern on call—who, by the way, called security on me when I wouldn't go away. Needless to say, I stood my ground even with security breathing down my neck. The only reason I wasn't tossed out was because I used the weight of the DCFS and my role as the head social worker on the island.

"A different nurse gave me the number for the head psychiatrist, but she's yet to return my call. I waited outside the locked unit, but no matter what I tried, they refused to let me in. My hands are tied. The only thing I could think of was to call that young public attorney here, Matt Gruper. Filled him in and asked him to see what he can do for Irene, considering how fast her freedom was stripped away. She needs someone to speak for her. You know, Mark, sometimes I really hate how much this system works against the most vulnerable. And what really bothers me is knowing she's likely being pumped full of drugs to keep her sedated. How does that help her in any way?"

Mark didn't pull his gaze from her. She knew he had a lot on his mind. "I wish I had an answer for you," he said, then slid his arm around her and pressed a kiss to her head. She started walking with him to the house, arm in arm to the steps, which she started up, feeling him right behind her.

"You want to tell me now what was so important that you couldn't say it over the phone?" she said. "I can see it's weighing on you."

Mark pulled out his key and slid it into the deadbolt, then opened the door. Billy Jo heard a woof and stepped in first, greeted by both Lucky and Sarge, their newest addition.

"Good boys," she said. "Missed you." She ran her hands over both dogs.

"What are you two doing back here already?" Gail appeared in the hallway, dressed in blue jeans, a navy pullover, and a coat, her graying hair tucked behind her ears. "Was about to head over to my place, make sure everything is okay."

She heard the door close and the click of the deadbolt lock, which she hadn't expected. She looked back to Mark, who was bending to pet both dogs.

"Need to have a word with Billy Jo," he said. "Stay a minute, Gail, as this will concern you, too."

"Sure," Gail said, shooting Billy Jo a questioning look as she shrugged out of her coat but kept hold of her bag.

Mark took Billy Jo's coat and tossed it on the bench behind them at the front door, and Billy Jo toed off her sneakers before starting into the kitchen just behind Gail. Mark didn't bother with his cowboy boots; she heard his heavy footsteps behind her until he stopped at the island and brushed back his jean jacket to rest his hand on his hip, just above his holstered Glock. Billy Jo rested her bulky bag on the countertop.

"When I walked into the station after leaving the hospital," Mark began, "one of the military guys from the morning—Dion, he said his name was—was waiting in my office along with another man who also had that CIA vibe. They wanted my answer. My time to think was basically a few hours, and that time was up. I'm not ready to make a decision like this, because my joining their team means the island isn't protected.

"Although I have an idea of what they're asking me to join, I don't know anything. I'm putting together the pieces about a secret group. Whom do they report to? Who funds them? Who are they all? My training wouldn't happen here. How long would I be gone? But the main thing he said, which has been in the back of my mind for a while, is that I get up every morning feeling as if I'm always ten steps behind the bad guys. I don't have a face or a name to put to those bad guys. All I know is how much control they hold, with minions all the way down. I'm starting to wonder who the good guys are, and that's something I never thought I'd wonder."

Billy Jo had never heard Mark talk this way. She pulled out a high-backed stool at the island and sat down, and Mark glanced from her to Gail.

"He brought up a lot of things," he continued. "The other guy, Mike Smith, though I don't think that's his real name, he knew about all my roadblocks, including this morning with little Mila Palmer and her missing kidney. What pissed me off more than anything was hearing no one will be held responsible, because if or when paperwork appears, what it will come down to is the fact that the state has control over all her medical decisions. No court will go against the doctors who took her kidney or the DCFS, who were part of it. Her kidney was likely bought. Maybe, if I spent weeks or months digging, I'd find the illegal black-market site where organs are ordered and track down exactly how those organs suddenly appear in the system, from the blood type to the age of the child, exactly as needed.

"I'm tired of it, Billy Jo. It seems this evil is so deeply embedded in society, in everything, and I'm only scratching the surface." He shrugged, then let his gaze linger on Gail. "He brought up Tolly and your son, Richard, and what those evil motherfuckers did to gain his compliance. I'm sorry we never talked about what happened and what it took to get Tolly to look the other way while they played their games right under everyone's noses. Worse, no one saw a thing. I never asked you what happened to Richard, but I'm asking now."

Billy Jo didn't have to look over to Gail to know she was likely poleaxed. The tension had ramped up. Mark let his gaze linger on the baby she carried before letting out a heavy sigh. He was good at hiding things, but not that good. He was worried.

The silence lingered. Gail's lips were pressed firmly together, her arms pulled over her chest. The heaviness was thick in the air, the reality of an ugly world that had always remained so intangible.

Gail nodded. "What do I know about any of my kids? I thought I knew them so well only to realize they have as many secrets as Tolly did and I had not a clue. Tolly never told me anything. After it came out that Tolly had been acting as the eyes and ears of predators, I spoke to Richard and asked him what happened. Richard said only that two cops had shown up and taken him from school, said his dad had been hurt. He went with them. How could he not? He was only eleven. He was tied up, gagged, locked in what he thought was a dark trunk, and photographed naked. He was terrified.

"He said he didn't know how long he was there, though it seemed like forever, before his dad opened the trunk and held him, asking him if he was hurt, wrapping a blanket around him. As Tolly took him home, he said he couldn't tell anyone, not even me, or the bad people would come back and do even worse to him and us. I can't believe Tolly convinced him to keep a secret like that from me. I asked Richard outright if they hurt him in any other ways, you know…" Gail stopped talking and dropped her gaze to the floor, and Billy Jo found herself looking over to Mark. The way his gaze softened, she knew he was likely thinking the same thing she was.

"Richard wouldn't share much," Gail continued. "Just said they'd kept him in that dark trunk and that it was hard to breathe. He was sure they were going to hurt him, kill him or something. He was just a terrified little kid. He said he wasn't surprised when he heard what his dad had done, as the pieces had fallen together for him, but the nightmares still haunt him. What hurts more than anything is that the last time I spoke with Richard before he sold his place on the island and left, he said he wished his father hadn't sold his soul to the devil. He said Tolly should have let him die, because he could never forgive his dad for choosing him and sacrificing all those kids. He blames me, too. Maybe because I never figured it out." She let out a sigh.

Billy Jo knew that Gail's kids hadn't called once since she'd moved in with her and Mark. She wondered at what point they'd stop condemning Gail for not seeing what none of them had, either.

"I'm sure he'll come around," she said. "When was the last time you talked with your kids?"

Gail offered her a weak smile that didn't reach her eyes. "Graham, Tolly's son from his first marriage, is the only one I've spoken to. He emailed me a photo of Trish's baby boy. She won't call. I didn't even know she'd had her baby. He'll be six months old now, and she's never told me anything about him. Apparently, Graham is the only one who doesn't blame me. Lori moved to Houston, and Richard is now in Denver, I know.

"I'm sure their feelings are more about what their father was involved in than about me, even though Tolly did it to get Richard back. How does one come to grips with the reality that he sacrificed so many children to save ours? I'm thinking that's why Richard is having such a hard time, knowing he got to live at the expense of so many others. So those men knew something about what happened to Richard? That's all I know, Mark, but I'm wondering if they approached you because they know you could be a target, as well. Ever wonder how many other cops or sheriffs have been made to compromise and look the other way?"

Mark lifted his chin and glanced away, and it was in that second that Billy Jo realized there was something else.

"Mark, what's going on?" she said. "Did someone threaten you? I know when you're spooked or something is off."

He was shaking his head as he stepped around the island to her and ran his hand over her shoulder. His touch always grounded her, but it didn't today, and maybe he knew, as he pulled her close and pressed a kiss to her forehead. His arm was around her, but he let it fall away as he leaned against the island, still touching her. "This Mike Smith, one of the things he said was that these people won't hesitate to get to me through you and the baby. That's why, Billy Jo, I think the only way to protect you and our baby is for me to join this team. I don't want to be worrying every moment about where you are and what could happen.

But if I join this team, I don't know how deep this goes. I don't know how long I'll be gone. You understand what I'm saying? It seems I'm damned if I do and damned if I don't. Yeah, I've had that thought for a while, wondering who's compromised and who isn't. I've gotten an idea by looking county by county, checking who's not being arrested or prosecuted and who is."

This was exactly what she didn't want to hear. The baby kicked, and the sound of a vehicle outside had her stepping back and her heartbeat picking up. She heard car doors and frowned, and the dogs barked. Mark was already walking to the door, his gun out, and she followed.

At the door, Mark holstered his gun and had the dogs both sitting.

"Mark, who is it?" she said.

He glanced back to her. "Alarm company. I asked Lacy to send them out here to get the security system and cameras up and running on every door and window. I want it monitored day and night." Then Mark was out the front door, talking to someone she couldn't see. He wasn't just worried; evidently, he was already making plans.

"You going to be okay with this?" Gail said from just behind her.

What was she supposed to say? "He's right. I love that Mark makes people take him as he is. He can't be compromised. He's always been on the same page as me: Kids and animals must be protected. Gail, as much as I don't want him to go and do this and not be here with me every day, I have this feeling deep down that if he doesn't, something could be waiting in the wings to come at us. I don't have blinders on. I was never allowed to live in that world."

She pulled her arms over her chest, resting them on Mark's baby growing inside her, as she faced Gail. "And I would never want Mark to have to make the same choice Tolly did. He may not have said it, but I hear what he doesn't say aloud."

She shut her eyes, feeling the weight of everything, listening to the clank of a ladder, the patter of footsteps from the dogs. Mark was coming in the front door, and the heaviness that had settled over him again held the weight of all he carried.

"So when do you start?" she said.

He hesitated and made a face as he walked to her, slid his arms around her, and pulled her against him, kissing the top of her head, holding her so tight. "As soon as I take care of things around here."

CHAPTER
Seven

Mark pulled up in front of the small island police station and turned off his Jeep. He pulled his keys from the ignition and shoved them in his jean jacket pocket as he took in the tinted glass windows of the station. In his pocket was a card with Mike Smith's phone number, and his feelings on that left him anything but settled. He pulled it out and dialed the number, then put his phone on speaker.

"Well, what did you decide?" Mike said. The phone hadn't even rung.

"If I take this job, how long would I be away?" Mark said. "My wife is pregnant. I'm also down a man. I haven't gotten around to hiring a deputy, with every-thing that's gone on."

"We need only a yes or no, Mark. I get it. We all have family and shit to do."

He wondered where Mike Smith was, and the other military guys who had shown up that morning. They apparently knew how to hide, even on a small island, which should have bothered him more than it did.

"I didn't say I wasn't interested. I have questions, is all. Taking this means I'm basically leaving the island unprotected, without its chief. That brings me back to my wife. I have no idea where I'm going, and as you said, I won't be able to share anything with her. How am I supposed to protect her if I'm not here?"

Mike sighed heavily. Mark didn't know why this was so damn hard. "Mark, let me be brutally honest. As long as these people in charge stay where they are, nothing changes. In fact, they're the ones behind the scenes, making everything you do so ridiculously difficult. They control the rules, and we all have to live by them, but they don't. These people will know how to get to your wife, your family, any way they can. You appoint someone you trust to take over for you. I'll make a few calls for you about a deputy and get someone there to keep the council appeased so your island isn't turned upside down.

"What you need to ask yourself is what future you want for your child. Come on, Mark. What you've seen so far, do you want that for your child? If you were killed tomorrow, you wouldn't be there to protect your wife or your kid. You want to go through all the what-ifs? I can list off a few dozen from your worst nightmares if you want. What if something were to happen to your wife? Sure, you have family for the baby, but you know as well as I do that if they want your child, they will take it any way they want.

"This evil that has operated unchecked runs more than anyone would ever admit. They are the deep state. They run the world. What if your wife is sitting at the lights in her car and is suddenly blindsided, killing her? What if your water is suddenly poisoned, or you have a gas leak or a break-in, or your wife goes for a home visit to a child in care and finds a gun to her head? What if your wife develops complications in labor and her doctor isn't available, but another one shows up and insists on an emergency C-section, and your baby is said to be stillborn and is taken away and never seen again? What if you or your wife wake up one day with a gun in your hand and the body of the other dead and no idea how it happened?

"You want me to keep going? I told you already they have six ways to Sunday to get to you, destroy you, or kill you. You know this. You've been stepping all over their toes and causing them an incredible amount of grief. I'm asking only once more: Are you in or are you out?"

Mark leaned his head back and felt the hand on his arm. He turned to Gail, who had been sitting beside him in the Jeep all along, so quiet. "Okay, I get it," he said. "But still, it's not going to be easy. The town council here has been gunning to put in someone who will look after their interests and be their lapdog, not the thorn in their side that I am."

"We know that. I'll make a call. You going to give me an answer or come up with more excuses? Look, we all have a reason we're doing this."

"I'm in," Mark said. "Tell me what's next." He jammed his hand in his hair just as Sarge whined behind him and licked his ear. Mark reached back to rub the dog's head, and Lucky nudged him for a pat as well. His dogs were sitting side by side in the back seat, becoming impatient.

"Get your ducks in a row," Mike said. "Make sure your family is taken care of. Appoint someone you trust to take over for you, but don't put your trust blindly in that one person. One thing the enemy does well is present themselves as your friends, your allies. Someone will call you tonight and tell you where to go, and you'll be debriefed then. And, Mark, one last thing: You made the right choice."

He shook his head, still holding the phone. "Wasn't really a choice, now, was it?"

"I'll see you later." Then Mike hung up. Of course, he hadn't answered.

"He's right, Mark, if you want my opinion," Gail said. He knew she had one foot out the door already, hinting every day about going back home.

"I need you to stay at our house with Billy Jo while I'm gone," he said. "Can you do that?"

The sadness that lingered in Gail's eyes had stolen the teasing light that had once been there. "I can," she said. "What are you going to say to the council? You know they'll insert their own person here who will do as they say, looking away from certain crimes and going after others you never would've."

Why couldn't everything be easier? He gave his door a yank and stepped out, taking in the heavy clouds and what looked like more rain on its way. He pulled the seat forward. "Come on, you two," he said, and both dogs jumped out and were at the door to the station as Mark gave the Jeep door a shove closed. "You think I don't know that?" he said. "Listen, I'm dead serious. I want you here in the office every day to keep an eye on everyone and everything. I'll see what kind of call this guy makes."

She was already shaking her head. "Mark, you and I

both know the minute you're gone, I'll be walked out of here by the council."

That feeling was back, the feeling of barely holding on to everything. He didn't have control. "You leave that to me," he said. "You just be here, because I need to know at least one person has my back." He wiped his hand over his face.

Gail nodded. "Whatever you need, Mark. You sure Billy Jo is going to be okay with this?"

His breath fogged in front of him, and he fisted his hands, feeling the cold. "She asked me when I was going, didn't she?" he said.

But he knew Billy Jo would never tell him no. She needed him, and maybe that was another reason the knot inside him was twisting. He stepped up on the sidewalk and opened the door to let the dogs in first, and they headed right over to Lacy, who was just coming out of the back room.

"Hey there, you two," she said.

Mark spotted Carmen at her desk, just hanging up the phone, and glanced back once to Gail as she unzipped her dark brown fall coat. He had everyone's attention as he took in the empty desk that had once belonged to him, the deputy position that had never been filled. He wondered what kind of call Mike was planning on making.

"I want to have a word with both of you, Lacy and Carmen," he said. "I'm taking some time off, not sure how long, but while I'm gone, Carmen will be running things here for me. Gail is going to be here every day to help with that. I know the position for deputy hasn't been filled, and I keep meaning to get to it…"

He wasn't sure what to make of Carmen's expression, how her brown eyes widened and she was shaking her head. "What are we talking here, a few days?" she said. "Wait, is something wrong with Billy Jo? You want me to be acting chief?" Her voice squeaked on that last part.

He shook his head. "No, Billy Jo is fine. I'm going to be away on a special assignment and will be off island. I've been offered a position. I'm not sure exactly how long, but it could be weeks, a few months. I'm not sure."

The quiet unsettled him more than anything.

"Does this have anything to do with the men who were in your office earlier?" Lacy said. Leave it to her to figure it out.

"Something like that," he replied. "I can't say any more. Carmen, are you up to it?"

She frowned and shrugged. "Sure, I can do it, but what about the council? When they come in here and throw their weight around, Chief, you know how to stand up to them. Not sure showing them the door will work out as well for me."

He knew she had a point, and he glanced back to Gail, who understood so much more about this island than he ever would. "You just handle things here for me," he said. "I'll deal with the council. You have any problems, you talk to Gail."

The phone was ringing, and Lacy was already reaching for it. Lucky had curled up in his dog bed, and Sarge was lapping up water. Mark took in how on edge and uncomfortable Carmen seemed.

"Mark, you should go through the cases you're working on with Carmen so she's up to speed," Gail said. "Then you need to tell the council." She walked around him, over to the empty desk that at one time had been his, and rested her coat and bag on it.

He took in his glassed-in office and gestured to Carmen. "Yup. Come on, Carmen," he said. She started walking into his office, and Mark followed, but he stopped beside Gail. "You know I trust you, right?"

Gail looked up at him. "You know, Mark, I have three kids, but you're more of a son to me than my own," she said. Then she tilted her head toward his office. "Go. You don't have a lot of time."

Lacy was gesturing to him. "Sure, I'll let the chief know," she said, then hung up. She had an odd look on her face. "That was Heather, the interim mayor. She said there's a new deputy who will be stationed over here, arriving tomorrow, while you're away on your special assignment."

Just then, Mark's phone dinged, and he pulled it from his pocket. The number was one he didn't recognize, and the text said, *New guy arriving tomorrow, Deputy Raul Booth. Called in a favor. Oh, and that new mayor? She's nice. —Mike*

Gail hadn't pulled her gaze from him. He showed her the text, then said, "Thanks, Lacy," as he shoved his phone back in his pocket and started walking into his office.

Carmen closed the door behind him. "Okay, Chief, it's just you and me. How about you tell me what's really going on?"

Mark went to stand on the other side of his desk as Carmen pulled her arms over her chest, the tension thick. "I've told you all I can. I've been asked to join a task force. It's important, Carmen, or I wouldn't be going. I don't know how long I'll be gone, and I can't tell you any more than that. A new deputy by the name of Raul Booth is arriving in the morning. I know nothing about him, so use your discretion. And I want you to lean on Gail. You'll be fine."

"That's all you can tell me? This is crazy, Chief."

Mark looked down at his desk, which was organized and familiar. "I need you to do me a favor," he said. He knew he hadn't answered her.

She made another face and shrugged. "What?" she said. There it was, the snark he knew came from a place of being scared and unsure.

"I need you to keep an eye on my wife. Gail is still at our place and will stay there, and the alarm company will get the entire system running and online. There's a monitoring station, so if there are any problems, you know, a call will come in here."

She angled her head and frowned. "You expecting trouble? Now you're freaking me out."

"I have no fucking idea what to expect, Carmen. So I need you to keep an eye out for my pregnant wife and drop in at her office often. Can you do that for me?"

Carmen uncrossed her arms and pulled in a heavy breath, then let it out. "Yeah, I can do that."

You missed your appointment today.

Billy Jo took in the text from her midwife as she strode into the bedroom, where Mark was packing a duffle bag on the bed. There had been way too much going on. She silenced her phone and set it on the nightstand. It was dark outside, and she could hear Gail loading the dishwasher after dinner, chicken and a side salad. She was already feeling a distance with Mark, which bothered her more than anything.

"Everything okay?" He gestured to her phone.

She shrugged. "Fine, just an appointment I missed today, with everything going on."

Mark reached for two sweatshirts in the closet and tucked them into the duffle bag. "Anything important?" He let his gaze linger, and she wondered and worried about the weight he carried.

She shrugged. "Nothing I can't handle tomorrow."

Mark pulled open the dresser drawer and retrieved a handful of t-shirts and socks. "I know we haven't had a moment to talk. All this has come out of left field, and you have to know how uneasy I feel, leaving you right now."

She did, of course, but it seemed as if her whole life had been about living on the edge, never being comfortable. She eased her way down onto the edge of the bed, resting her hand over their baby, Mark's baby. "I'll be fine. You talked with this Mike Smith? Can you tell me anything else, like where you're going, what you'll be doing?" She fisted her hands. "This may sound selfish, but why does it have to be you?"

But she already knew the answer. He was the best, her handsome, rough-around-the-edges, uncompromising, and flawed husband.

"You want me to call them and say no?" he said.

She realized he'd do it for her, but she shook her head. She couldn't look at him. She already missed him even though he was still there.

He let out a sigh and walked around the bed, and the mattress dipped as he sat beside her. "I need to know you're protected. Yes, I talked to Mike. I don't know any of the details except that I'm flying to Idaho, training there. I'll be debriefed and will have to sign a military NDA along with everything. I won't be able to tell you any of the details, but I'll call you every day. I'll make sure the first thing I do is establish a way for you to get a hold of me." He leaned forward, his forearms resting on his knees, and he let out a heavy sigh again. "The alarm is hooked up, and I want you to make sure it's always on. Don't forget, not ever. You let the dogs outside, and you make sure the second they come in, you have it turned back on. You have a gun in the safe. Make sure it's handy. You know my rifles are in the gun case downstairs along with ammo. Gail is staying, and I can call my mom and dad and ask them to come out, or your parents. You know they'd drop everything in a minute to be here."

She slid her hand over his arm. "You mean to be invading my space? Don't worry, I know how to work the alarm, and Gail and the dogs are here. I don't plan on using your guns, Mark, but in the event of an invasion, I know how to aim and pull the trigger. You just worry about you and making sure nothing happens to you. You think I don't have an idea what you're doing, Mark? I'm not a fool. I know this is bigger than you and me. I just wish it didn't have to be you. The only thing that will make this easier is knowing you're in some way trying to make this world safer for our baby."

He really had the most amazing vivid blue eyes, and she hoped their baby would be lucky enough to have his red hair, too. She really hoped so.

"I want you to promise me while I'm gone that you won't overdo it," he said. "That you'll rest, eat well…"

She flicked her gaze up, pulling in a breath as he reached for her hand.

"Hey, I know you. Because of that right there," he said, softly tapping her chest where her heart was, "you give everything of yourself to everyone, Billy Jo. But right now, doing what I need to do, I can't be worried that you're overdoing it or taking chances. Promise me you'll make sure you put yourself first. Pass off what you can to Lisa. And I also need you to promise me you won't ever be alone. Make sure someone knows where you are at all times." Now he was coddling her.

"I'm not going to jeopardize this baby, Mark," she said. "I'll rest and take it easy, but I'm not an invalid, and I still have kids who need me in their corner. How about this? You promise me you won't take unnecessary chances, and I'll do the same."

He shook his head. The phone was ringing from the kitchen, and she was sure Gail answered. Evidently, time was up.

There was a tap on their open door. "Hey, Mark, it's for you," Gail said and handed him the phone.

He stood and reached for it, and Billy Jo pushed off the bed and followed Gail out of the bedroom, into the kitchen.

"You know who was on the phone?" Billy Jo said.

Gail closed up the dishwasher and then gave the counter a wipe with the sponge. "No idea. A man, could be anyone. Mark asked me to show up at the station every day, keep an eye on things. You know, Billy Jo, I'm really proud of Mark and what he's doing, but it's left me disillusioned because my own husband chose to play both sides. I know he did it for our son, but Richard can't even stand to be around me because of the choice his father made. I wish a lot of things, one of which is that maybe Tolly could have had just a little of what Mark does. What would Mark choose if his back was against the wall? His child or a deal with the devil?"

It was a thought she didn't want in her head. She had rested her hand on the high back of the stool when she heard her phone ringing from where she'd left it in the bedroom. She could feel Gail watching her as she hurried there. Mark was still on the phone and glanced back to her as she reached for her phone and saw the name of the hospital.

"Hello?" she said as she stepped out of the bedroom, watching Lucky lapping up water from his dish.

"Is this the chief's wife?"

Billy Jo didn't recognize the voice. "This is Billy Jo McCabe, yes. Who is this?"

"I'm calling about Irene, Irene Palmer. You left your card with the head nurse in Psychiatry. You wanted to see Irene, and I know you were denied."

"I left my number for the psychiatrist in charge to call me back."

"She won't call you back," the person said. "She knows you called. I saw what happened. Irene is in isolation. She's sleeping and will likely be that way for a few days, pumped full of antipsychotics and then some, leaving her completely out of it. She won't be able to talk, think, anything. I heard the psychiatrist say she was extending the emergency hold for twenty-eight days. You should know she hasn't even seen Irene, but that happens here. She'll be kept drugged. It's a cocktail of tranquilizers that leaves a person catatonic. The hospital has the authority to keep that little girl from her mother. And I heard the doctor say something, too, that she's tired of problem mothers thinking they have a right to a kid. I heard that a lawyer called, and the head nurse spouted off about you causing all kinds of problems."

Billy Jo felt a hand on her shoulder, and there was Mark, though he pulled it away and walked over to Gail. "You didn't tell me your name," she said. "Who are you? You work at the hospital?" She glanced back to Mark again. He gestured to her phone. Of course, he wanted to know who she was talking to.

"I'd rather not say. Me phoning you puts my job in jeopardy. Look, I don't know why I called except that I heard the talk about the little girl already. She was in the care of the state, and her kidney was taken out. Heard a few say you were really upset and wanting to see Irene, and you didn't agree with the doctor taking her daughter away. Is that true? Are you really fighting to keep them together?"

She didn't know who this woman was, and she sensed her lack of trust. "I wasn't there when Mila was taken from her mother," she said. "I never would have okayed it. From what I saw, Irene was upset. I'm not sure I would have acted any differently."

No, she'd have buried them and maybe let her husband loose on them, knowing he'd have put one or all of them six feet under if that were their child. But then, Billy Jo had a family of pit bulls behind her, so that never would've been her. Not now, anyway.

"So Matt was there?" she said. "He's a lawyer. I called him to see what he can do for Irene."

"Nah, he didn't show. Just heard he called. Was told Irene was in isolation and wouldn't be able to see him. Don't think he pushed. He only left word to have someone call him when she wakes up. Look, I have to go. I just wanted to tell you, if you're expecting the doctor to call you, she won't. Not sure there's anything you can do for Irene or the kid, either."

Billy Jo sensed the woman was going to hang up. "Please wait! Can you meet me?"

There was silence. "No. I shouldn't have called. I have a family. I can't get involved."

"But you did call. Please, what's your name? Just meet me. I promise it'll be just between you and me. No one will know."

"I'm sorry, I can't, and I'd appreciate it if you'd keep this call to yourself. But if you want to help her, be the squeaky wheel. Call the doctor every day. Show up here. Demand to see Irene, and get that lawyer to demand to see her. She'll be all doped up, so you'll need to question everything, ask what she's on and why. They'll try to blow you off, ignore you, so you'll have to push. Schedule an emergency hearing with a judge, but only after she's not pumped full of tranquilizers. They'll try to say she's dangerous, and the judge is going to believe the doctors, administrators, and nurses. They'll dummy their records, even make something up to justify what they've done. I hope you'll do it, but too many don't. I've got to go." This time, she did hang up.

Billy Jo turned to Mark. Gail was now in the living room, shoving wood in the woodstove, both the dogs with her.

"Who was that?" Mark jutted his chin to her phone, and she knew her overprotective husband was only moments from being gone.

"Just something I have to handle tomorrow. What about you?"

He let out a heavy sigh and pulled his hand over his forehead. "Plan's bumped up. I need to leave tonight. In an hour." He walked right over to her and pressed both his hands to her shoulders.

"It was supposed to be the morning," she said.

He looked past her, and she felt her eyes burn. Damn, she didn't cry! She pressed her lips together, and he must have known, as he pulled her closer to him and held her, pressing a kiss to the top of her head.

"I'm sorry," he said. "I love you."

She knew he did, but it didn't help or make it easier. As she held on to him, it suddenly became too real, what he was leaving to do. Billy Jo rested her palm on his chest and pushed back, looking up at him, wiping a tear she'd tried not to shed. "I know. This sucks."

He ran his hand through her hair and then settled it over their baby. "You look after yourself and our little one," he said.

She covered his hand with hers, just holding him there for a moment as she said, "Always."

Nine

It was pitch black outside as Mark sat in the back of the club cab pickup. He knew it was close to midnight, but he didn't have a clue where they were. Somewhere in Idaho, the middle of fucking nowhere.

"So how much farther?" he said to the man behind the wheel, who wore a wool pullover and jeans. He was pretty sure he was military, but which branch, he didn't know. What was his name again, Gopher?

"A couple miles. So I heard you have a pregnant wife. How many kids?" It was the other guy in the passenger side who'd spoken. He had dark hair, wavy, with a scar on his left cheek, and he had quite the twang. He was older, around Mark's dad's age. Jasper Roberts was his name, Mark knew from the brief meeting when he'd stepped off the float plane that had docked at a lake. It really was the middle of nowhere, a part of the state he'd never been.

"Our first," Mark said.

"Ah, got three myself. Two from my first marriage.

Been married a few times. Gopher, you radio in?" Jasper said. Something about him made Mark figure he was in charge. He reached for a walkie-talkie and said, "We're coming in. Open the gate."

As they rounded a bend, the headlights flickered onto what looked like a twelve-foot fence with barbed wire at the top. Someone opened it, and Mark was very aware of the isolation, the heavy forest, the unpaved backwoods road. He cringed at every rut they hit, as the truck was taking a beating. He took out his cell phone and saw absolutely no service.

"This really is out in the middle of nowhere," he said.

"You're not worried, are you?" Jasper said without looking back at him. Then he did, and Mark wondered whether he was serious or had a bad sense of humor.

"Hell, yeah," he replied, "considering I have no fucking idea where I am. I have no cell service, and I don't know either of you, where we're going, or who's there. You know, all that common-sense shit your parents pound into you? Pretty sure horror movies have been filmed about this very thing, the dumbass who thinks he's saving the world only to walk right into the enemy camp and be taken out."

There was silence. Then both men burst out laughing.

"Mark, I think you're going to fit right in," Jasper said, turning again to look back at him in the darkened cab.

Just then, the dirt road opened up, and he saw lights and what looked like a warehouse with trucks and SUVs parked out front.

"The team will be waiting. Everyone is here," Jasper

said as he opened his door, and Mark opened his as well and stepped out. He reached back for his bag, feeling the chill in the air. His breath fogged, and he spotted an industrial glass door from which a man walked out, dressed casually, wearing blue jeans and a heavy dark coat.

"Thanks for picking up, Mark," the man said. It was Mike Smith. Mark recognized him from his voice. "We have a few administrative things you need to take care of and sign, and then we can get right down to business. We have a little team meeting happening, so you can meet everyone."

Mark was having trouble with how fast this was evolving. He needed a second to catch his breath, but that second was just more time away from his pregnant wife. He shook Mike's hand. The other men were already gone, though he had no idea where. Mike had him walking to the heavy industrial glass door. The big sign at the top of the concrete building said AVIS AIR.

"So is this where I sign an NDA and you fill me in on what's going on?" Mark said as Mike held the door for him. They walked into a well-lit lobby with gray slate floors and a desk with a man behind it. Security? Maybe.

"No time to waste," Mike said. "We'll get the paper-work out of the way so we can get started. Stanley, buzz us in."

The security guy behind the desk was dressed in all black, black jeans and a black turtleneck, and a holster over his shoulder held a gun. He leaned forward and pressed something, and a door buzzed. Mike pulled open the heavy dark wood door, and then Mark was walking down a hall side by side with him. They passed two offices in which stood men in military fatigues.

Mike gestured to an open door. "In here," he said. "You can put your bag down there." He pointed to a metal chair. In the office was a man with brown hair, military cut, in military fatigues, behind a computer screen. Papers were on the desk, and Mike was saying something to the man, who was now standing, tall and fit. Mark didn't have a clue what this place was.

"First things first, Mark," Mike said. "A military NDA. Read it and sign it." He slid over to him the first of many papers. Mark lifted it and scanned the legalese as a pen appeared, held out to him by Mike, who said, "You're seriously going to read it? No one reads everything. Let me sum it up for you. You talk about anything we do here or share any intelligence of any kind, including operational info, classified information, or any details of operations and your life as you know it will be over. Understand?"

Mark took the pen. He realized Mike's surfer hippy look, with his long wavy hair, only hid someone a lot more serious. He took in the door, still open behind him, and leaned down to the desk. He flicked the pen and pressed the ballpoint to the line above his name, then pulled in a breath as he scribbled his signature. He dropped the pen on the desk, and the paper was quickly pulled back and another slid in front of him by the military man who seemed to be organizing all this.

"This is your ID," Mike said, handing it to him. "Pay will be deposited directly in your account, and you'll receive benefits, etc."

Mark reached for the pen again. He realized he'd never thought of any of this. He took in what looked like a pile of paper he still needed to sign. "So I get paid for this, and benefits?" He reached for the badge, an ID with a different name.

"Your ID has your name as Mark Miller. When in the field, you'll take nothing with you that says who you really are, Chief of Roche Harbor, Mark Friessen, son of Jed and Diana and husband to Billy Jo."

The military man held a computer tablet out to him. "Thumb and fingers here," he said.

Mark had never seen this kind of fingerprinting. He pressed his thumb and fingers to the screen, and the military man punched something into the keyboard, so meticulous.

"Yeah, you'll have benefits," Mike said. "If something happens to you, a pension will go to your wife, though it's fuck-all. If you're injured or killed in the line of duty, on a mission, your family will never be told what you were doing. This isn't a get-rich scheme, but what you're doing here is serving your country and taking down the enemy that has walked among us. Just so you know, this operation doesn't exist on paper." Mike gestured to the ceiling and then the open door. "Sign everything, and when you're done, Sergeant Beatty here will bring you down to the situation room, where the team is waiting. Then we can get started."

Mike didn't wait for him to say anything, ask anything, or change his mind. He was already out the door.

"Sir, sign here." The sergeant handed him another paper, holding out a blue pen to him.

Mark leaned down, staring at the endless papers, and said, "You want to summarize any of this?"

The sergeant shook his head. "Sorry, sir. That's above my pay grade."

Mark stared for a second, realizing he was serious, then flicked the pen, read the fine print, and signed.

MARK FISTED his hand after signing what had felt like a hundred pages as he followed the sergeant around the corner. The man had taken his cell phone, wallet, and gun, leaving him feeling as if he'd been stripped naked.

The sergeant stopped at a steel door with a keypad. He punched in numbers, pushed it open, and said, "In here, sir."

Mark wondered whether he'd ever get used to being called sir. He stepped into a room that held a long conference table and at least a dozen men sitting around. His gaze went to Mike in the corner, then to Dion, then to Gopher and Jasper, who were leaning against the wall.

"So this is the new guy," one of them said.

"Mark, glad you could join us," Mike said. "I want you to meet Raven Douglas. She's running this team."

A woman only a few inches taller than his wife stepped forward. She had dark hair and a round face, wearing blue jeans and a long-sleeved navy shirt. Her hair was pulled back, and her eyes were light brown. "Mark, good to meet you," she said. "Starting to my right, this is Flint, Evers, Jackson, Freidman, Moya, Bankman, Slovie, Knightowl, and Baldy. You remember Gopher and Jasper, who picked you up. Over there are Mike Smith and Dion. Okay, let's get started. Mark, sorry, but you're going to be playing catchup."

A few were already sitting, and Baldy, who happened to be bald, with a beard and a solid build much like Mark's, slid a chair out for him and patted it before shoving it toward him and saying, "Sit your ass down, newbie."

Mark grabbed the chair on wheels and slid it over to the table to sit down just as a screen lit up the entire wall behind Raven. He wondered how everyone fit in. Who was in charge, Raven? Mike Smith still stood off to the side with Dion. A lot of players. The room darkened a bit as he took in a map.

Raven was pointing to a spot in Wyoming. "This is an aerial view of a private ranch owned by tech giant Rudolph Hughes. It's fifteen-hundred acres. New intel has come in regarding an elaborate tunnel system under the house. We have human trafficking, and all indications from our military assets point to a baby mill being run out of there. It's heavily guarded, a fortress, with electronic surveillance and what looks like his own private army."

"Hang on a second, here," Mark said. "What are we talking about, babies, children, women? How many? And you really mean the billionaire Rudolph Hughes?"

"Anywhere from thirty to one hundred, and yes, he's very wealthy," said a light-haired man at the end of the table. What was his name, Evers? He was lounging in a chair, lanky, older, and it appeared he hadn't shaved in a week. The accent, too, was different. Mark was trying to place it. French, maybe?

Mark dragged his gaze back to Raven, feeling the knot tighten. He leaned back, resting his elbow on the arm of the chair. For a moment, all he could think was a blinding *What the fuck!* He realized his hand was suddenly up, and everyone was staring his way as he said, "Okay, evidently, you all know way more than me, but are we really talking the same Rudolph Hughes who's in partnerships with many world governments? Our government? What the hell? What is he doing?" Mark was positive his voice had squeaked. This was crazy.

"It's a mindfuck, isn't it?" Baldy said, turning in his chair with a look that appeared far too calm. "Wait until we drag you down the rabbit hole with us and you learn about all the families, the big names, tied to this."

Mark didn't have a clue what to say.

"Okay, everyone, short and sweet tonight," Raven said. "Just be ready. We head out at first light, so get some sleep. Mark, hang back a second."

Chairs scraped as everyone rose. Mark was trying to understand what the hell this was. It was that feeling of once again being a rookie, on the outside looking in. A few hands slapped his shoulder as the guys walked past, and a few welcomed him to the team before making their way out. Then it was just Raven, and as the door closed behind him, Mark looked over to see Mike Smith had stayed behind, as well. He moved to get up.

"No, Mark, sit," Raven said. "You have that look everyone first has when they show up here. I get that you're a small-town cop and haven't seen things on this grand of a scale yet. Last week, we cleaned out a tunnel system in Pittsburgh under a home belonging to an old banking family."

Pictures appeared on the screen as Raven flicked something in her hand, and Mark took in images of cages, children, everything black and dark. His ears were ringing.

"We found dead kids, bones, the kinds of things nightmares are made of," she continued. "We lost two of ours in the raid. Former Sheriff Merrill Lee was one. It takes a chunk out of your soul. Another was done after the horror we found—chains, cages, and remains. You know what these monsters do to the young ones, the innocents? Human trafficking is what runs everything, and behind it is a world of elites who government leaders take their orders from. Think the deep state and everything in between.

"They torture these children. They're brought in from across the border, used in rituals, sacrifices, to satisfy the depravity of these sick Satanist fucks. You need to get your head straight, because every time we go in, some of the kids we find can't be saved. Think of a wild animal who has never had human touch or contact. Some of the women we rescue are also too far gone after what's been done to them. Mike, you want to add anything else?" Raven turned off the screen, and it was just a wall again.

Mark didn't know what passed between them, but Raven left, Mike holding the door open for her and closing it behind her. The ensuing silence didn't ease Mark's mind in the least. Mike Smith walked over and pulled out the chair Baldy had been sitting in, and he sat down and rested both his arms on the table. He seemed to be collecting his thoughts or something.

"Once upon a time, I worked for the CIA," he said, "and for the Department of Justice before that. I was a spook. I signed up because I wanted to make a difference. But one day I was appointed to the White House, and I found myself suddenly reporting to the chief of staff. I was in a world where nothing made any sense, knowing I could never talk about what I saw and heard.

"One day I was sent to his house. There were two secret service agents there, just outside the door. In the house, I heard something, a crying child in distress. I ran upstairs, and there were two other agents there. It was a very young child crying, pleading. I asked the agents what the hell was going on. I guess they thought I knew already. I tried to go past them, push past, but one grabbed me in a headlock.

"I was listening to the sounds of a child being burned in the shower by the chief of staff, who got off on it. He tortured a three-year-old, and I was forced to listen and do nothing. I will never get the sound out of my head. He killed the kid. The body was disposed of by the agents. I understand there was always another. What he did to them was something from a sick world, and there wasn't a damn thing I could do.

"I went to my boss in the CIA, and next I found myself in a concrete cell, beaten. They came at me with everything to shut me down. The only reason I walked out of there and am still breathing was because they believed they had my compliance. That was eleven years, seven months, six days ago." He lifted his wrist, looking at his watch. "I can give you the date right down to the second."

Finally, he looked straight at Mark. "Ever since then, I knew the monsters people believe hide only in dark shadows, the lowlifes and degenerates, are in fact living among us. They're the puppet-masters behind the scenes, running everything." He gestured to Mark. "We can't save them all, but one by one, we take down a deep state that has preyed on the innocent, sucking everything good from them. These degenerates are evil in ways you would never be able to get your head around.

"That property in Wyoming, the tunnel system, will have been funded by taxpayers. It's yet another playground for these sick motherfuckers. These parasites have built a worldwide network, and no two are the same. All I can tell you, Mark, is we take them out, arrest some bad guys, and save those we can. These guys we arrest aren't even the middlemen, though. They're way down the totem pole, just like that doctor you took out, and the priest. They follow orders and are replaceable. You take out two, and three more are recruited to take their place.

"I do this for that three-year-old I couldn't save. His name was Benny Castillo. He disappeared from North Texas. His father was a janitor, his mother a grocery store clerk. He disappeared from daycare, and there were no leads. The parents are now divorced. The mother remarried and moved to New Mexico, but the father still lives in that same small town, putting flyers up for his missing son."

Mark didn't have a clue what to say. "Why haven't you told them? You evidently found out about the family. How?"

Mike flattened his hands on the table and then let out a heavy sigh as he leaned back in his chair. He shoved his hands in his pockets, and his blue eyes held an edge that now made a little more sense. "Tell them what, that their three-year-old son was kidnapped and raped and tortured by a man who works next to the most powerful man in the world? He's a sadistic pedophile, yet he's out there in front of news cameras, revered by the people as a hero and someone to be looked up to. There would be no justice. All I'd be doing was signing their death warrant, because what parent would sit back and do nothing? And these are not the kind of people you can go after and live to talk about. Nope, I wouldn't do that to them, but I do keep an eye out. It's like your first kill. It sticks with you, haunts you…"

He pushed away from the table and stood up. "Come on. I'll show you where you're bunking down. Tomorrow will be your first mission, and you've had no time to get your feet wet. We're throwing you right in the deep end, but you wouldn't be here if I didn't think you could do this. Mark, if I can leave you with one thing, it's that what you saw under the house of that priest was child's play compared to what we'll be walking into." Then he pulled a cell phone from his pocket and tossed it on the table. "Your new phone. Call your wife on it; it can't be tracked. Breakfast is at oh-five-hundred. Any questions?"

Mark figured that was rhetorical, but he said, "Just one."

Mike frowned.

"Who's in charge, you or Raven?"

Mike pulled his hands from his pockets. "You have a question, you bring it to me. Anything operational comes from Raven. As for who we report to, well, that's classified," he said. Then he was walking to the door and yanking it open, and all Mark could think about was how much he missed Billy Jo.

CHAPTER
Ten

"Strong heartbeat," the midwife said. "Listen to that. Wow, everything looks good. Baby looks good. So we still need to talk about where you want to deliver. Have you and your husband had a chance to discuss? I know you said not in the hospital, but you have some options—at home, a water birth…"

Billy Jo pulled down her light brown maternity sweater and sat up. "I will not be having this baby in the hospital, not a chance. I'll have it at home."

The midwife's long dark hair was pulled back in a ponytail, and she wore black yoga pants and a purple long-sleeved tunic. As she put away the fetal monitor, she tossed Billy Jo a curious look. "At home is fine," she said. "You'll be more comfortable, too. You know, I haven't met your husband yet. After three visits, I kind of expected him to show up."

What was she supposed to say? Billy Jo had never told Mark she was seeing a midwife, not because she believed he would have a problem with it but because she herself was trying to let go of her beliefs that doctors were the only way.

"He's away right now, but you'll meet him before the baby is born," she said. "Most people tell me having a baby is a medical condition that has to be treated in the hospital. Try to tell someone you're considering having a baby at home, and they look at you as if you've lost your mind."

Her phone dinged from beside her, and Billy Jo practically landed on it as she slid off the exam table. It was only a text from Lisa. Maybe her anxiety was because she still hadn't heard from Mark. She'd sent two texts with only silence in reply.

The midwife's lips quirked in amusement. "Has that happened to you?" she said. "Someone told you that you were crazy? Or are you struggling with your social conditioning and the idea that doing something outside the norm is crazy?" She nodded toward the phone. "You have something important there? You look a little on edge."

"No, just work. Nothing that can't wait. And no, I've told only one person about seeing you. I guess it's my own beliefs I'm struggling with," Billy Jo said. And her lack of trust, but she figured she'd keep that to herself.

"Ah, I see," the midwife said. "Well, that makes a lot of sense. Women have been having babies since the beginning of time, but having babies in the hospital is a Western thing that really started around the Second World War. I think, last I heard, about ninety-nine percent of women now have their babies in a hospital. Although more seem to be seeking out midwives lately, there's still a stronghold of Western medicine domi-nance, with money being funneled there. Sure, if a woman is at high risk and her health is bad, she needs to go to the hospital, but for the majority who are healthy, a home birth and a midwife is better on both mom and baby. That's as long as you keep doing as well as you are, sleeping, eating right, getting plenty of rest, and having no stress. You plan on working right up until you have the baby?"

That was something else she and Mark had never talked about.

"I promised Mark I wouldn't overdo it, but I plan to work as long as I can, right up until this baby is born."

The midwife only nodded. Billy Jo reached for her bag on the chair and took a second glance at her cell phone and the message from Lisa before stuffing it in her purse: *Pam says the hospital called. They're releasing Mila Palmer. They want her picked up by a social worker and turned over to the state.* Billy Jo thought she swore under her breath as she shut her eyes for a second.

"Remember, Billy Jo, stress isn't a friend when you're pregnant," the midwife said. "Pass off anything you can. Take it from me: This is your first. If you want to have the baby at home, you and baby need to be healthy."

She held up her phone. "Passing this off would only give me more stress. Thanks, Deborah. When do you want to see me again? I need to go take care of this." Billy Jo reached for her blue fall coat and shrugged it on, lifting her brown hair, which was well past her shoulders, over the collar.

"Four weeks, unless you notice anything that doesn't feel right. If you do, and I mean anything, you call and come in," Deborah said.

Billy Jo nodded. "Sure. Just text me when you can schedule me in. I have to run."

She pulled open the door and stepped out of the exam room to the empty front of the office, and she was already calling Lisa as she stepped outside into a light rain and flicked the fob to unlock her car.

"You got my message," was all Lisa said.

"Yup. So the hospital is done with Mila, and now, because they've basically kidnapped her mother and fucked her over, we have to find a home for her? Mila was free for only how many hours, forty-eight?" She really could add nastiness to her tone better than anyone.

She pulled open her car door and tossed her purse onto the passenger seat as she slid behind the wheel, then pushed the seat back, wondering if the baby had grown in the forty-five minutes she'd been in the midwife's office.

"What do you want me to do?" Lisa said. "The hospital is releasing her. I can make some calls and find her an emergency placement."

Billy Jo pulled her door closed, the phone still to her ear. "No, that poor little girl has been through hell. As long as she's here, I'm going to make sure she doesn't end up somewhere that will further traumatize her. I'm on my way to the hospital now. Just tell them I'm coming. But in the meantime, can you see what you can find out about other family, a relative or someone related to the Palmers? There has to be something you can find. Can you do that?" Billy Jo put her key in the ignition and started the car.

"Sure, I'll call you with what I find," Lisa said, then hung up.

Billy Jo backed out of her spot and pulled onto the main road, feeling tired because she wasn't used to sleeping alone. She'd never expected to feel as connected to someone as she was to Mark. Damn, did she miss him. Maybe that was also why her mood was so sour.

She arrived at the hospital in fifteen minutes and pulled into an empty spot at the end of a row, then reached for her phone and thumbed through her contacts until she landed on the public defender's office. She dialed Matt's direct line.

"Matt Gruper." He had a low voice and always sounded so distracted.

"Matt, this is Billy Jo McCabe. I'm calling about the Palmers. Remember Irene and how I asked you to do something to help her? Were you able to? Because I just got a call from my office that the hospital has demanded we come and get Mila."

There was silence on the other end, then a heavy sigh. "I called but couldn't talk to her."

Billy Jo shut her eyes. Why had she thought Matt would be all over this? "No shit, Sherlock. She's locked in a psych ward and pumped full of tranquilizers and God knows what else. She's likely comatose and drooling. Do you have no fucking idea what they do to you in a psych ward?" She really was going right for the jugular today. She could almost hear Mark, knowing he'd have been giving her that look of his, telling her to dial it way back.

"What do you want me to do, Billy Jo? I'm a lawyer. To help a client, I have to be able to communicate with her. I need to talk to her or, better yet, to the psychiatrist."

"Matt, the head psychiatrist isn't going to call you or me. Last night, I heard from someone who works there. The head psychiatrist, without even seeing Irene, has extended her stay another twenty-eight days. I'm here at the hospital now, and I plan on raising holy hell until I get face to face with the psychiatrist. I called you so that you would show up and be a pit bull for Irene. Do I need to remind you what happened to Mila in the care of the state all because Irene challenged a doctor? It's horrifying, the amount of power doctors have. Mila has lost more than half her childhood since being taken from her mother. So I want you to get your ass down here and show some damn backbone, because I have to figure out how to make sure Mila isn't made a ward of the state again. If that happens, Irene may never get her back. Do I need to remind you that Mila was returned minus a kidney?"

Mark wasn't there to dig into the case for her. For the first time since marrying him, she really felt on her own.

"Okay, I get it," Matt said. "Don't do anything stupid. I'm on my way."

When he hung up, Billy Jo let out a breath. She fisted her hands before pocketing her phone and yanking open her door to step out into the rain, but her phone buzzed again, and she dropped her keys to the ground as she retrieved it and saw an unknown number. *Damn, Mark, why haven't you called?* She hesitated only a second as she leaned down and picked up her keys. "Hello?"

"Hey, how are you?"

Billy Jo pressed her hand to the door as she stood up. "Mark? Where are you calling from? Are you okay? I called your cell a few times." She wanted to tell him so many things. She wanted to feel his arms around her.

"I'm fine, just busy, is all," he said. "Sorry, I have a

new number while I'm here. Got in late and was thrown into the middle of things. I wanted to give you a quick call before we head out. I'll send you a text with this number. Call it if you need to get a hold of me, day or night." He let out a sigh, and she wasn't sure what she was hearing in the background. "You sleep okay?"

She shook her head. "I'd sleep better if you were here. Any idea yet how long you'll be gone? You get weekends off or anything like that?"

"Ah, sorry, babe, I don't know. I'm kind of scrambling, getting my footing here, but I'll try to call tomorrow, and as soon as I know what's what, I'll call you. Try to get a nap in today, and don't do anything I wouldn't want you to. Any more word on the Palmers?"

Billy Jo stared over at the hospital, knowing Mark wouldn't want her doing what she was about to do. "Yeah. They want to release little Mila this morning. I'm about to go and talk to the head psychiatrist here. Matt's on his way, too, so hopefully he can work some magic, but at the end of the day, Mark, if this little girl ends up back in the system, this could be it for her."

A pickup, an older model, was pulling into the parking lot, and she realized it was Matt.

"Mark, he's here," Billy Jo said.

"Okay, go save that little girl, but any trouble, you call Carmen. I do not want you going head to head with anyone right now."

"Hey, don't worry about me. You just worry about yourself."

There was silence again, and she thought she heard voices in the background. "Look, Billy Jo, I've got to go. I love you, and worrying about you is what I do." Then he hung up before she could add anything, like "I love you, too," or "Don't you dare get shot or killed." The text came through with the number and a smiley face, which was unlike him, along with the message *Be good. Tell our baby that Daddy loves him or her.*

She squeezed her phone and tucked it in her purse as Matt stepped out of his pickup. He was tall, lanky, and in a suit that appeared way too baggy. She took a second and rested her hand on the baby. "Your daddy misses you. He loves you," she said, and it was then she felt the baby kick.

The first person she saw as she walked through the doors of the ER was Marshall Collins. She tapped Matt's chest again, taking in how young he looked. She knew he was twenty-seven only because she'd asked, but she swore he could've passed for eighteen, easy.

"That's him," she said, "the ER doctor responsible for this mess. We have him to thank."

He was talking to a couple of nurses, laughing about something, wearing blue scrubs with a white coat pulled overtop, his conservative dark hair appearing far too neat for a doctor in a busy ER.

"Billy Jo, what is the objective here?" Matt said.

She thought for a moment that he sounded scared. She stopped and faced him, her coat unzipped, her bulky bag slipping off her shoulder. She slid the strap back up. "Matt, do I need to walk you through this? It's simply to get Irene out of here and get the ER doc and shrink to back off or, better yet, admit they made a mistake so that mom and daughter can be reunited. I do not want this girl back in the system."

He had light brown eyes and a narrow face. The only reason she could tell he was any good was that he knew how to shut up and listen. "I get that, I do," he said, "but isn't she already back in the system?" He angled his head, perceptive, picking up way more than people gave him credit for. "You didn't file the paper-work, did you?"

For a moment, she felt on the spot. Out of her peripheral, she caught Collins walking their way. "I'm stalling as long as I can," she said just before he joined them.

"I heard the hospital called you about Mila Palmer, and she's ready to go," he said. "Pediatrics have reported that all tests came back, and she's good. Doesn't appear to be any damage."

"You mean other than the fact that her kidney was stolen from her?" Billy Jo was so done with the way no one was addressing the greatest crime, in her book.

The doctor let out a heavy sigh.

"I understand you're the doctor who saw both Irene and Mila last night," said Matt. "Matt Gruper, lawyer. I'm with her." He gestured to Billy Jo, who wondered where he was going.

"Oh, okay," Collins said. "Well, it's tragic, what happened. But the little girl is doing well. She'll just need to rest and take it easy for a little bit. I believe they were discharging her this morning, so you're here to pick her up?"

Billy Jo shook her head. "Actually, we're here to see Irene," she said, "you know, Mila's mother, who was trying to protect her and is now locked in the psych ward. Because of your call, that little girl will go back in the system and be placed in a temporary home. They'll give her a bed and meals, but that's it. She's still recuperating. How do you expect her to heal when she's been ripped from her mother and placed with strangers who don't give a shit about her? She's going to be terrified. How can someone, let alone a child, take it easy when she's scared?"

She felt a hand on her shoulder, Matt's. The ER doctor lifted his hands in the air, and she thought he would step back and walk away. Apparently, he didn't like confrontation.

"Billy Jo is right," Matt said. "A mother came to you to find out what happened to her daughter. I think it was a bit of an overreach to hold her in psych. I understand the psychiatrist, without even looking at Irene, extended her stay another twenty-eight days. How does that work?"

Billy Jo blinked. She'd mentioned that in passing, so maybe Matt had listened more than she thought.

"Look, we're all busy," Collins said. "I'm sure Doctor Lapell, the head of psychiatry, had a reason."

"And what would that reason have been, exactly?" Matt was very direct. The only problem was that his baggy off-the-rack suit didn't give him credibility, in Billy Jo's opinion. Maybe she'd have a talk with him about his appearance. That was just something she'd picked up from her dad, who'd drilled into her that appearances mattered, especially for a lawyer taking on any authority.

"I don't go around questioning fellow doctors and

their decisions," Collins said. "Look, I'm sorry. This is a shitty situation, and I feel bad for Irene."

"Is it?" Billy Jo said. "Because I'm getting the impression that you may have overreacted, and instead of fessing up to making a mistake, you're digging in. Is that what you're doing? Because I can tell you, if I were in Irene's shoes, I may not have been as nice as she was."

Doctor Collins seemed to pull back. The look he leveled her with wasn't that of someone seeing reason. In fact, she was bringing the worst out in him. She'd never been a good negotiator, preferring to go right for the jugular.

"She threatened my staff," he said. "She was loud, disruptive. She couldn't be reasoned with, and I had cause to believe she was a danger to her child and to the staff. I stand by my decision. Now, if you'll excuse me, I hope you'll do your job, at least, and see to it that the little girl is placed somewhere safe." Then he walked away, and as Billy Jo went to take a step to follow, a hand slapped to her shoulder.

"Nope, you're not doing that," Matt said. "He's done talking, and he walked away. Save that fight for Irene. You really don't have any idea how to win someone over?"

Somehow, Matt had her walking the other way, around the corner and to the elevators, where he punched the button to go up. Billy Jo gripped the strap of her bag, knowing she'd never been able to paste a smile on her face and pretend everything was okay.

"Sorry, it's one of my faults," she said. "I've never learned to be nice to someone when I really want to scratch his eyes out."

The elevator opened, and Matt held the door as she stepped inside. He pressed the button for the psychiatric floor. "Well, one of the things I was warned about you is that if you don't like someone, they'll know it. I guess you never learned how to use empathy, understanding, kindness…"

She wondered what kind of look was on her face. Matt let out a heavy sigh, then looked up to the floor number display and shook his head as the door opened.

"You want me to be understanding to an arrogant jerk?" she said.

Matt was still shaking his head as he held the door for her again, and she stepped out of the elevator. He followed. "How about you let me do the talking? Because I have to tell you, if you pull that, wanting to bash heads with the psychiatrist, Irene is likely never going to get out of here, and her daughter's outcome will be bleak. I'm pretty sure judges aren't too keen on giving children back to parents who've found themselves committed to the psych ward."

She knew he was right. "Fine, but don't let her push you around or blow you off."

He said nothing as they walked over to the nurses' station in front of the locked door to the psych ward. A nurse with a nametag reading *Melinda* was behind the desk. Her hair was light brown and in a tight bun.

"Hi," Matt said. "Melinda, is it? I'm Matt Gruper. I'm an attorney for Irene Palmer. I know you're really busy right now, but I'm wondering if it would be possible to speak with Doctor Lapell, the head of psychiatry. I called last night."

He sounded almost flirty. Billy Jo just stared at him,

then dragged her gaze to the nurse, who was standing and reaching for an iPad.

"I can have her paged," Melinda said. "Who did you say the patient was?"

Billy Jo found herself staring at the locked door, wondering who had called her. Evidently not Melinda, who had the phone to her ear and was dialing.

"Irene Palmer," Matt said. "She was brought up last night."

The nurse was shaking her head, looking at the screen. "Yes, I have a lawyer here who represents Irene Palmer and wants to speak with Doctor Lapell. Can you page her?" she said. then hung up, and Billy Jo nudged Matt and gestured to the door. He frowned and shook his head.

The phone rang.

"Psychiatry," the nurse said as she answered. "Yes, Doctor Lapell, he's right here with a woman." The nurse let the phone slide away from her mouth. "What are your names, again?"

"Billy Jo McCabe, social worker," Billy Jo said, "and this is Matt Gruper, Irene Palmer's lawyer." She couldn't help herself, and she wondered by the nurse's frown if she already knew who she was.

"A social worker and a lawyer. Oh, I see," Melinda said into the phone. "Sure, I'll let them know." Then she hung up, already shaking her head. "I'm sorry. The doctor isn't available right now, and unfortunately, if you're here to see Irene, she's in isolation. There was an incident last night."

"An incident?" Billy Jo said. She felt the hand on her shoulder again.

"Billy Jo, I got this," Matt said. "What incident?"

The nurse dragged her gaze between the two of them and lifted her hands. "I'm not sure. The doctor said only that there was an incident last night with a nurse and Irene refusing meds."

Billy Jo already knew what that meant. She found herself stepping away, hearing the back and forth as she reached for her cell phone from her bag and dialed.

"Roche Harbour Police, this is Lacy."

"Hey, Lacy, it's Billy Jo. Who's there, Gail, Carmen...?" She looked back to the desk. Matt was listening to something the nurse was saying.

"Both are here. Carmen has the new guy, Raul Booth, in Mark's office. She's feeling him out, I think. Do you want me to get her?"

Billy Jo ran her hand over the back of her neck and shook her head. "No, put Gail on. Thanks, Lacy." She didn't have a clue what Matt was saying to the nurse, but at least he was still talking.

"Where are you?" Gail said as she came on the line.

"At the hospital. Matt Gruper is here with me. I think I screwed things up already for Irene, as I couldn't bring myself to grovel to the ER doctor who put her here. I think the shrink is avoiding me, Matt, all of us. Can't get into the locked psych ward, and I think I've stalled all I can about little Mila. They want to discharge her. I have Lisa looking for any other family, but having the psychiatrist release Irene and sign off that she's not a danger would be better." Billy Jo let out a heavy sigh. "Mark called, too. He's got a new phone, but he couldn't talk long."

"What can I do?" Gail had a way about her that really did make Billy Jo feel better.

"Short of making her talk to me?"

Gail laughed. "Let me see what I can do. Just stay there. No matter what, don't leave."

As Gail hung up, Billy Jo turned to see Matt walking over to her.

"Try as I might, we're not getting in," he said. "I was told to try back later."

Billy Jo heard the ding of her phone and took in the text from Gail: *Hang tough. Carmen and the rookie are on their way.* Not what she'd expected, but she could live with that.

"We're not going anywhere," she said. "Carmen and the new deputy are on the way. Come on, Matt. You need to pull on your big-boy pants and play hardball. We're not leaving until we talk with the psychiatrist, see Irene, and get her the hell out of here."

Matt said nothing.

Billy Jo walked over to the nurses' station, Melinda tracking her every move. "Just so you know," she said, "if we have to wait here all day, we will, so call the doctor back and tell her to stop hiding. This isn't a game. Committing a woman who was only protecting her child, then doping her up and then extending her stay without even seeing her, doesn't make you just a bad doctor but also a shitty human being."

She heard Matt groan.

The nurse reached for the phone and dialed, and Billy Jo looked to Matt, ready to say, "See? I told you so," when she heard the nurse say, "This is Melinda at the fourth-floor psych ward. I need security up here."

Billy Jo dragged her gaze back to the nurse. The woman was staring long and hard at her, the phone to her ear, nodding.

"That's right," she said. "Yes, send two. They said

they're not leaving." She nodded again, and Billy Jo wanted to rip the phone from her hand. "Thank you," she finished in a voice that sounded far too happy. Then she hung up and lifted the flat of her hand to Billy Jo. "Uh-uh, not doing a battle of wills. Security is on their way, so you can leave now or deal with them."

Mark was trying to get his head around where they were going. The men on this team, he'd learned, were from all over. Along with him, there was a former Oklahoma sheriff, an Alaskan deputy, two former Navy SEALs, a former marine, someone from the French Army Special Forces, and a former Canadian intelligence officer. Then there was a former CIA agent, one whose resume had also included time in the Navy and then as a private contractor.

For the life of him, Mark couldn't shake the feeling that he was the least qualified person there. He was geared up in military fatigues, carrying what felt like a mountain, with a rifle across his lap, a sidearm, and more ammo than he thought he'd ever need. He rode stuffed in the middle of the back of an SUV, following a Humvee that carried the rest of the team. His earpiece was in, and his mic was on so he could communicate with everyone. His head was spinning as he thought of what they were walking into.

"You've been pretty quiet there, newbie," said Baldy

from beside him. "Let me give you the advice I wish someone would have given me: Don't get stuck in your head. We have a job to do, in and out. You're going to see some things from your worst nightmares. We don't know who's down in those tunnels. They go on forever, crisscrossing the country and the world. I've seen things down there I wish I hadn't in places your family would never believe exist."

Mark glanced to Mike, who sat in the passenger seat up front and seemed to always have an eye on him. "I don't understand this tunnel thing. Why tunnels? Who built them, and why?" He was still trying to get his head around all the images he'd seen, the maps that showed an intricate tunnel system.

"For moving product," Baldy said. "Believe it or not, they're built by one of the military agencies using contractors. Human trafficking, harvesting of adrenochrome and organs from children, takes place underground, out of sight. It's elaborate. Just think of what it takes to run something of this magnitude. There are many, many teams out there, Mark, doing what we're doing, saving these kids, putting an end to something that has gone on forever."

Mark said nothing. In the distance was a huge estate, and out front were two military vehicles, an SUV, and what he thought was a white tent being set up, though for what, he didn't have a clue. The vehicle stopped, and Baldy stepped out, as did Dion from the other side beside him. Mark followed, his rifle loaded and ready. He was about to check it again when a hand touched his shoulder, and Mike fell in beside him as he followed the team to the house, the double doors wide open. He realized a local sheriff was also there inside.

"Hey, Mark, just hang back a second," Mike said. "There's no way to get you ready for what you're about to walk into, so you and I are going to take the rear. I'll be behind you."

Mark only nodded, taking in the tent. Someone wearing some type of hazmat suit flicked it open and walked in, and Mark nodded toward it. "What is that?"

Mike didn't look over. They kept walking through the double doors. Past the kitchen, the local sheriff stood by what appeared to be a door in the wall, which was open.

"Specialists for the kids," Mike said. "Don't worry about it. Hope you don't get claustrophobic. Damn, I hate these."

Mark watched the team head through the open door one by one. It appeared to have been hidden in the wall of a study, covered by the same matching gold and red wallpaper. He did a quick check of his rifle, the safety on, the rounds ready. Spiral stairs went down, lined by concrete walls, dimly lit, with the scent of something he didn't want to get used to.

Then he heard voices. His heart hammered as he stepped down to an area with soft lighting and what looked like a small theater with a stage. He had his rifle up, very aware of how empty the place was, holding the feeling of something dark and ugly. He looked for anything or anyone as the men of the team moved through another doorway by the stage.

He heard the first *pop* and then another. Gunfire.

Mark was hurrying behind Dion, who was pressed to the wall, glancing past the open door, into the darkness, his gun up, ready to fire.

"Clear, clear!" someone shouted, and Dion hurried in.

Mark stopped, running on pure adrenaline. He flicked on his headlamp and moved into the dark room, hearing that *pop, pop* again, hearing his breath and shouting. When a light flicked on, he spotted blood and two bodies, one a man in scrubs, the other a woman, dead, on the ground.

He was standing in what appeared to be a nursery, with what he thought had to be fifteen babies. Everything about the place seemed like a hospital.

There was more gunfire, and he moved through another open door, another hallway, more rooms.

"There are babies here! Who's shooting?" someone called out. It was him, he realized. He hadn't meant to speak out loud.

"Keep going," yelled Mike from behind him.

Mark kept moving with the team. In darkness again, he spotted a flashbang, and Dion, off to his right, was kicking in another door. In his peripheral was a man, a gun, and Mark just fired—twice. Everything went into slow motion. He had hit the man square in the chest, and as he went down, Mark took in everything: the short dark hair, the uniform that of the US Army.

There was a tap on his shoulder. "Hey, it's clear." It was Mike.

Mark didn't ease his grip on his rifle as he took in the young man lying dead and the tunnel that seemed to go on forever into darkness. "Shit... He was military."

"He's on the wrong side, Mark," Mike said. "A stupid kid. Likely didn't even know it. Shake it off. Over there." He gestured, and Mark spotted flashlights in another hallway, all concrete.

An awful racket sounded ahead, and soon Jasper pushed past him from the darkened hallway. "God fucking dammit, Mike!" he shouted. "These sick motherfuckers! I need some air…"

Mark kept going. His flashlight shone over concrete and rock, then steel. The rest of the team were spreading out down the concrete corridor, though how far it went, he had no idea. He shone his own flashlight over steel cages stacked three high, and the light flickered over the face of a child, dirty, with tangled hair. His heart was hammering. When he went to touch the cage and open it, a hand landed on his arm to stop him. The child shrieked like a wild animal and lunged, banging the door, reaching through.

"No, no, no, don't touch," Mike said, lifting his own flashlight in the darkened corridor of cages.

Mark realized he was looking at children, a lot of children, stuck in cages in the dark. He realized now that nothing could have prepared him for what he was seeing. "We have to get them out," he said.

"Okay, listen up, everyone," Raven called out. Mark had forgotten she was in the lead. "Moya, Bankman, Friedman, Slovie, you're on rescue. The ones you can save, wrap them in a blanket and move them out. The rest in the nursery…"

A hand landed on his shoulder again. "You and me. I want to show you something," Mike said, then motioned for Mark to follow him back out into the open corridor where the young army kid was still lying dead. What had he been doing, guarding the door he'd come out of?

Mike opened it and stepped inside, and a light

flicked on. It was steel, sterile, holding an autopsy table and more medical equipment than Mark had ever seen.

"You remember that little girl you spoke about with the missing kidney?" Mike said.

Mark figured it wasn't a question he was supposed to answer. He watched the former CIA officer pull open a large walk-in cooler that held boxes and portable coolers, racks and shelves.

"There's everything here, from hearts to kidneys. On the black market of child organ harvesting, organs are shipped to some buyers within hours. Everything is labeled and marked by blood type, genetic match, and the age and gender of the child. You have blood, too, with adrenochrome. It's a drug the elites love for its psychedelic and life-extending properties. You know how they do it, right?"

Against the reality of what he was looking at, he couldn't get his tongue to move. "They put children through extreme fear and trauma to get adrenaline into the blood. I've heard about it. I just never imagined seeing it."

Mark stared at the life that had been lost.

"How many more places like this?" Mark said.

Mike shook his head. "Too many, and they're not all like this. Last week, we had to wade through the bodies of dead children. You know what happens. This isn't pretty. Screams echo for me every time I walk into these places, even when the kids are dead or saying nothing. It's as if their souls are screaming out for justice, for someone to care, to do something. I suppose that's my gift or my curse. It's as if that fear, that evil, is now part of this place. You see what I was talking about? What you found on your island is small-time compared to this."

Mike tapped one of the boxes and then seemed to collect himself. "We're going to save the kids we can, but you need to understand, Mark, some of those children have never been touched. Some of them were born down here for this and have never seen the light of day. One of the mistakes we made when we started over two years ago was to bring up a child who had always been in the dark. They don't survive. The babies in there were born from trafficked women. Those doctors we shot, as far as I'm concerned, got off too easy."

Mike turned away and started back, gripping his rifle, slinging the harness over his shoulder and neck and adjusting it again. "This is going to be all day, Mark, and into tomorrow and the next. We take up the kids we can, wrapped in a blanket to keep the light off them, to the hospital tent. Then we'll spend the next days searching out these tunnels for anyone or anything still hiding down here. Keep your eyes open, because where we are is where the boogeyman really lives. Then, after we've done searching, we get to blow all of this up so no one ever gets to use it again."

"You do realize who I am, right?" Billy Jo said. She had never been one to use her position, but right now, she couldn't shake the feeling that everyone was following a script. From the elevator appeared two men from security, one tall and lanky, with light hair, and the other with dark hair, not as tall. They looked as if they spent more time sitting than doing anything else. Their shirts were white, with gold badges pinned to their chests, and their pants and ties were black.

"Ma'am, you're creating a ruckus, and you've been asked to leave," one said. "Now, are you going to go peacefully, or do we need to call the police?"

Evidently, they had their marching orders, which didn't include putting pieces of the puzzle together.

"Billy Jo, let's just go," Matt said from beside her. "This isn't accomplishing anything."

She wanted to snarl as she dragged her gaze over and up to him. "Man up, would you? There's no way we're leaving. At least I'm not." She turned back to the security guard and leaned in. "Go for it. Call the police," she said, feeling the fight that had always been part of her.

One of the security guards pulled cuffs from a pouch on his belt, and she stared in horror as the other grabbed her arm.

"You're not putting those on me," she said, but the one pulled her arm back, and the other slapped on the cuffs.

"Hey, hey, what are you doing?" Matt jumped in. "Take those off! She's pregnant. Are you crazy?"

Billy Jo had her cheek pressed to the wall when she heard the ding of the elevator. Both her wrists were cuffed behind her back, and she felt the pinch as a hand pressed into her shoulder. She turned, the hand still on her, seeing her bag on the floor. She hadn't even known she'd dropped it. She was feeling too many things at once, picturing her husband and wishing he were there.

"She's been asked to leave, and so have you," one of the guards said. "The police have been called. This is a hospital and private property. You want to go out in cuffs, too?"

The hand was on her arm, above her elbow. Then the elevator door slid open, and there was Carmen. Beside her was a man with brown hair, not much taller than her, with the start of a beard, wearing a fall coat over a brown deputy shirt and badge. Carmen said nothing, just narrowed her gaze as she headed over, her hands on her duty belt.

"Good timing," the guard said. "Was just bringing down this troublemaker—and the other one, too."

Carmen angled her head, taking in Billy Jo's hands

cuffed behind her back. The man with her had to be the new deputy. He appeared confused, taking them all in.

"You put the chief's pregnant wife in handcuffs?" Carmen said. Damn, she sounded so calm.

Billy Jo still felt the hand on her shoulder, the other on her elbow, as if she were dangerous. After a second of silence, no one saying anything, she turned her head to Carmen and bit out, "You took long enough getting here."

Carmen gestured for her to turn around. "Take those damn cuffs off her, would you? Man, I would not want to be you when the chief finds out."

"Look, I had no idea she was the chief's wife," one of the security guards said as he removed the cuffs. "Just got a call about people causing a disturbance."

Billy Jo wrapped her hands over her wrists, feeling the new deputy watching her. His eyes were light brown, and she didn't have a clue what to make of him.

Just then, a door from the locked unit opened, and a woman asked, "What's going on here?"

Billy Jo glanced over to who she thought was a doctor, wearing a white coat over a blouse and purple wool skirt that went to her knees. Matt had his back to Billy Jo, speaking with her already.

"We haven't met," the deputy said to Billy Jo, holding out his hand. "I'm Raul Booth. Didn't have a chance to meet your husband, but I've heard all about him."

She wasn't sure if it was a twang or a drawl she heard. She hesitated only a second before taking his hand, his handshake strong, firm. His hands were callused.

"So what are we supposed to be doing here?" he

said, more to her than Carmen. The two security guards were walking into the elevator with, she thought, their tails tucked between their legs after a scolding from Carmen.

Carmen touched her arm. "You okay?"

Billy Jo shrugged. "Sure. Just had my pride kicked out of me, is all. I can't believe they cuffed a pregnant woman. Two tough guys, trying to throw their weight around…" She didn't know what to make of the exchange between Raul and Carmen at that. Her anger had her heart racing, which wasn't good for the baby.

"You two have met, I take it," Carmen said, gesturing between Billy Jo and Raul, who appeared to be taking in everything around them, trying to figure it out.

"Has Gail filled you in about Irene?" Billy Jo said. "And that's Matt Gruper, a lawyer I called for her. Not sure who he's talking to."

Carmen was already heading over to Matt and the doctor. Raul gestured for Billy Jo to go first. He wasn't strikingly handsome, but he had a vibe she suspected the ladies would flock to.

"After you, ma'am," he said.

"It's Billy Jo," she said. "I'm not anyone's ma'am." She hadn't meant to snap. As she took a step, Raul followed, shaking his head.

"Just a show of respect, is all," he said. "It's how I was raised, ma'am."

She knew she made a face. Raul reached for her bag on the floor before she could, holding it out to her. So he had manners, too. She took the purse and said nothing as they joined Carmen. Everyone was now looking at her.

"Billy Jo, this is Doctor Lapell, the head of psychiatry," Matt said. "Doctor Lapell, this is Billy Jo McCabe. She's the social worker here. As I was saying, we're here to see Irene Palmer."

The woman had reddish brown hair pulled back in a stylish bun, glasses, and brown eyes. She was shaking her head. "And as I was saying, Ms. Palmer is in no condition for visitors. She is heavily medicated and, I suspect, suffering from mania."

Billy Jo felt herself leaning in. "Mania? So you saw her, then? I was here yesterday after she was brought up, and I'm not sure how you could come up with a diagnosis in less than twenty-four hours, especially when she's been kept basically tranquilized and asleep, completely out of it—or, as you said, medicated."

The doctor was looking right at her, and so was everyone else. For a moment, she didn't think she'd answer.

"Doctor Lapell, we're not visitors," Matt said. "I'm a lawyer, Irene's lawyer, here to make sure her rights are not being violated. Do I need to get an order before a judge to make you let us in?"

The doctor's gaze landed on Carmen. "Fine. You want to see her?" she said. "Don't stay long. Melinda, buzz us in."

The door buzzed, and the doctor was already walking toward it and pulling it open. Matt and Carmen followed. Again, Raul seemed to hang back, waiting for her to walk ahead of him. He reached for the door and held it for her.

"So, Raul, where did you come from?" she said.

The door closed. An orderly in white scrubs sat beyond it, and Billy Jo took in the sterile hall. In a room off to the right were tables and chairs, patients sitting around a TV. The nurses' station was behind a glass window. Nothing was open.

"Recently, or growing up?" Raul said. He didn't walk in front of her but slightly behind. There was something comforting about him and his awareness, his way of taking everyone and everything in.

"Well, the accent," she said. "Start there, your family, whatever you want to share."

His lips pulled up in an easy smile. He glanced over to the closed doors along the hall, and she wondered who was behind them. In the open rooms were just beds and nothing else. "Grew up in southern Appalachia, bordering rural Tennessee," he said slowly, deliberately.

"Don't know much about that area," she said. "That's a mountain range, isn't it?"

It was a poor, mainly white region, she knew, with poverty the likes of which few understood.

"Yes, with mountain people," he said. "Not many folks even know we exist. My father always said no one ever considers the dirt poor. We certainly wouldn't make the history books. It was a life of hard work, back breaking, until corporate America came in and took what wasn't theirs. Timber and mining companies…" He narrowed his eyes, and she figured there had to be a story there.

"I had no idea. Never met anyone from there. Your family still live there?"

He dragged his gaze from one room to another across the hall, then to Billy Jo. "My grandfather had twenty acres, which went to my father and his two brothers. Only my father's piece is left, just over five acres. Most of my family still lives up there. Got four sisters, seven brothers, and, at last count, twenty-six nieces and nephews. But some scattered when our land was taken. My two uncles lost theirs due to back taxes or some bullshit. The land was picked up by corporate big names, absentee. It's just owned and gone. Some seventy-five percent of land up there is now owned by just ten companies.

"Fifty percent of all the county land, too, was given to the timber and mining companies. It was all about profit, getting the resources the hills are known for. It was something few knew about, but we did. We were called uneducated hicks, white trash, but all the way back to my grandparents, we knew more than any researcher about what was really going on. We knew who was making changes for their own benefit, families that took what wasn't theirs and bled this country dry with their corruption. Not the answer you were looking for," he said. "These lost souls, you sure this is a battle you want to take on?"

He was deliberate and fascinating, and she thought there was more to his story. An orderly was now at a door ahead of them, unlocking it. The doctor held a chart and lifted the papers on it.

"Yeah," Billy Jo said. "Irene's got a little girl she was fighting for. It's scary, really, that if you fight the wrong people, you can end up in here."

Raul had a steady gaze. He nodded toward Carmen. "That's nothing new. Just more folks have eyes now, I suppose, to see it."

Billy Jo wondered whether he meant her or was alluding to something else.

He tapped her arm and said, "Hey, you need to take a look. I don't think you're going to be talking to her."

Billy Jo stepped through the open door, the orderly standing just off to the side. Matt and the doctor were in the small room already. Irene wore blue pajamas, lying on a cot with no sheets or bedding of any kind, with restraints on her ankles and wrists. She was staring straight ahead, and her eyes fixed on Billy Jo. She was drooling on the bed, and her nose was running as if she were silently crying.

"Irene, I'm Doctor Lapell." The doctor leaned down and flicked a penlight over both her eyes, one and then the other. She shook her head. Irene was trying to say something, but it was just a slur of words she could barely form. "How long ago was she given the Aripiprazole?" Doctor Lapell said, looking past Billy Jo to a nurse in scrubs with a brown sweater pulled overtop.

"One of the residents gave it an hour ago," the nurse said.

The doctor was shaking her head.

"Full-on antipsychotic," Raul whispered to Billy Jo, leaning close. "Would say they pumped her full of it. Nasty stuff."

She frowned, glancing up at him.

"You ain't getting her out of here like that," he said. "Figure out another angle—or a miracle."

Matt was talking to Irene, but she wasn't listening, and he stepped back. Billy Jo didn't know what made her look, but she glanced back out into the hall, and two doors down, a nurse with dark hair, pushing a cart, opened a door and then looked right at her. A strange feeling shot through her, one she couldn't shake.

"I'll be right back," she said to Carmen and Raul.

Billy Jo walked down the hall to the room the nurse had gone into, a storage closet. She caught the door before it closed and stepped inside. The shelves were stocked with linens, boxes, and medical supplies, and the woman was reaching for a box of rubber gloves and a stack of towels.

"I'm Billy Jo McCabe, a social worker," she said.

The woman looked right at her and let out a heavy sigh. "I know who you are."

Billy Jo nodded. The voice was one she'd never forget. "You called me last night about Irene."

The woman lifted her hands and shook her head. "I don't know what you're talking about."

"I think you do. I recognize your voice. I'm good with voices. Look, I haven't told anyone about you, and I don't plan to. I'm just trying to get a woman out of here who shouldn't be here. You're a nurse?"

The woman rested her hands on the shelves. Billy Jo knew she was pissed off. She shook her head. "Don't make me regret calling you," she said. "Yeah, I'm a nurse. You getting her out of here? I see you managed to get Doctor Lapell to show up. How?"

Billy Jo furrowed her brow. "So she hasn't seen her yet? But she's been diagnosed with mania. How does that happen?"

The woman, whose name she didn't even know, made a face. "You think she's spent any real time with half the people in here before getting them diagnosed? Nah, it seems to be the desired thing, calling it mania when nothing else will fit. Lapell just signs off on what she's presented and has the residents figure it out. Heard it took two orderlies to hold Irene down and pump her full of that shit... Will take a few days once she's off it before she can talk, then a while before she can think again."

There was a tap on the door, and it opened to reveal Raul, taking everything in. "There you are," he said. "The lawyer is done. Thought you should know the doctor is leaving, as well." He was holding the door.

Billy Jo glanced back to the nurse, who turned away, pulling supplies off the shelf and putting them on the cart. She knew she had nothing else.

Billy Jo started to the door, and Raul tracked her, taking in everything, holding the door as she slipped past him.

"You figure out your plan B yet?" he said.

She suspected he knew more than she thought. He walked with her, and she let out a heavy sigh and said, "No, but if you have any ideas, I'm all ears. Her daughter is about to be discharged, and if I don't have this figured out, then she's back in state care, and this time, I don't think Irene will get her back."

Carmen was leaning against the wall, her cell phone out, thumbing through it, and Matt was talking with the doctor just outside the door, which had been pulled closed by the orderly and locked again.

"Doctor Lapell, is it?" Raul said, approaching them. "I'm wondering how Ms. Palmer has been diagnosed with anything in the condition she's in. Pumping antipsychotics into anyone and then expecting to have a reasonable conversation is an interesting approach to diagnosing…mania, was it? Just wondering how that works, considering this is the first time you've seen Ms. Palmer. You picked a drug known to cause strokes. I'm wondering what the desired outcome is for you."

Billy Jo looked up at him. He had really emphasized

each word. She'd never heard someone talk so slowly, as if making every statement count.

The doctor frowned, and Matt narrowed his eyes, taking in Raul and then dragging his gaze back to the doctor. Lapell pressed her lips together and shoved her hands in her pockets. Even Carmen had pushed away from the wall. How did Raul know all that?

"I can't help thinking there's been an overreaction here," he continued. "Now, you've been a psychiatrist for how long?"

No one said anything. The doctor was standing in thick wedged high heels, tan, expensive leather, from the look of them.

"Look, yes, it's true this is the first time I've seen Ms. Palmer," she said, "but I've been doing this a long time, sixteen years. Been running this department for four. I do not toss out diagnoses lightly. Ms. Palmer was placed on a forty-eight-hour hold by Doctor Collins, and with the state she was in…"

"Excuse me. Didn't her hold get extended?" Billy Jo jumped in.

The doctor frowned, her hands still shoved in the pockets of that white coat Billy Jo had come to hate. "Forty-eight hours is not enough time to properly assess a patient. From the notes and what I was told, she was violent, angry, and had to be restrained. Now, from what I also understand, she's had a difficult time, and I suspect an undiagnosed history of mental illness. But with mania, there is a treatment. It can take some time, but a twenty-eight-day hold is necessary. Otherwise, she's a danger to her child."

Billy Jo could almost feel the doors closing for good on Irene.

"Well," Raul said, "now I'm curious, so maybe you could help me understand what a normal reaction would be for a mother who's just figured out that a medical procedure has been done on her child without her consent, that she was cut open, her kidney taken. To me, and this is just me, personally, I would think a mother should fight tooth and nail for her kid instead of being polite and mindful or okay with someone violating her child. My own mother, God rest her soul, would have marched in here with her shotgun and ripped anyone who did that to her child limb from limb. But then, I grew up dirt poor, kind of a hick, really, in rural Tennessee, where we didn't let strangers hurt our kids."

Everyone was looking at Raul, who pulled his arms over his chest. Billy Jo frowned. Carmen leaned in, too quiet.

"You know, it could be possible there was an overreaction," Doctor Lapell said unexpectedly. "Why don't I have another talk with Doctor Collins and see if we can't figure something out?"

Billy Jo's phone dinged, and she reached into her bag to pull it out. It was a text from Lisa: *Tracked down Irene's mother and sister in Jackson Hole, and Mila's father lives in Colorado. Do you want me to call them? The hospital called the office again and talked to Pam. She stalled them…for now.*

She turned away and texted back, *No, not yet. Still at the hospital. Just stall for a little longer.*

She got a thumbs-up in reply.

"Oh, Doctor Lapell," she said, "while you're speaking with Doctor Collins, I understand Pediatrics want to release Mila Palmer, her daughter, the little girl who had her kidney removed, yet no one is looking into that. I understand I'm expected to find a bed and a home away from her mother, who was just protecting her child. It would helpful if Pediatrics could decide to keep Mila another day or two while you all sort out this mess."

The doctor made a face. "I can't make any promises, but let me make a few calls," she said. Then she was walking away.

Raul tapped her arm. "Nice one," he said. She wondered if he was about to high-five her.

Matt said, "I'm going to tag along with her and make sure something else isn't cooked up. Just maybe we get Irene out of here without standing before a judge and jumping through legal loopholes."

Carmen watched as Matt walked away, then turned back to Billy Jo and Raul, who pressed his hand against the wall, leaning on it. "You know Mark would blow a gasket if he knew how we found you, cuffed by those security guards," she said.

Billy Jo let out a sigh and rested her hand over her baby, feeling the kick. "You're right, which is why you're not going to tell him." She dragged her gaze from Carmen to Raul, who had the most mysterious eyes, considering and watching her but saying nothing. "I want your word, both of you."

Raul shrugged. "Well, I never met him."

Carmen lifted her hands. "I don't plan on bringing it up, but if he finds out, Billy Jo, that I didn't tell him…"

Billy Jo slid her hand over Carmen's arm. "He won't find out. The last thing he needs right now is to be distracted."

Raul tapped her shoulder and gestured to Matt, who was walking back their way, lifting his thumb in the air.

"Good news," he called out. "They're dropping the

hold, and Mila isn't being discharged until Irene is ready. I guess the threat of being charged with medical kidnapping was not something they wanted to deal with, considering Irene suddenly has the new chief, a deputy, a social worker, and a lawyer asking too many questions on her behalf, questions they do not want to answer."

Mark's phone dinged, and he took in the voicemail notification, knowing it was from Billy Jo, just as Baldy slid a beer in front of him at the roadside bar where twelve of the sixteen members of his team had gathered for, as they said, a moment to decompress. They'd basically dumped him into the back of a pickup, telling rather than asking.

"Drink up," said Baldy.

Mark reached for the ice-cold beer, leaning against the bar in blue jeans and a navy sweatshirt. He didn't know a thing about Baldy other than that he appeared to be like a den mother for the guys on the team.

Mark took a swallow of the beer when his phone dinged again, and he lifted it to see his wife's text: *Just checking. Haven't gone to bed yet. Still up if you can talk?*

He put the cell phone face-down on the bar top.

"Problems?" Baldy lifted his beer, gesturing to Mark's phone and then to him before looking away.

Mark took another swallow of his beer, wondering how much he would have to drink to erase what he'd seen. "Just the wife," he said. He hadn't been able to make himself call Billy Jo in how many days, now? Five.

"You know, the marriage thing has been kind of tricky for me," Baldy said. "I've got a couple kids with wife number one, another with wife number two. Doing what we're doing here takes something out of a man. You're going to have to figure out a way to compartmentalize, put away everything we do, what you see, and hang on to the good you feel with your wife, or you're not going to make it. You did good out there. You got something on your mind, newbie?"

He wondered if the nickname everyone called him would ever go away. The bar was by no means packed, but the boys he worked with and had gone into hell with were doing shots, beer, and more rounds. Drinking himself to oblivion was not something he did, but he understood why they were.

"Is it always the same?" he said.

Baldy leaned back against the bar, looking right at him. He wore a gray t-shirt with the blue logo of some ball team, not a wrinkle on it, as if it had been freshly ironed. The tattoo down his left arm was of a dragon, with the ink of the long tail wrapping up around his bicep and over his shoulder. Mark had seen it once.

"Is what the same?" Baldy said. "You wondering specifically about what you saw, what we did, the country estate in the middle of nowhere, or the ones who didn't make it?"

Mark knew he made a face. He took in his phone again, feeling the distance from his wife, wondering whether he'd ever forget the child covered with a blanket whom he'd carried out and into the tent, a makeshift hospital. He'd been a Japanese boy, he thought, maybe two or three. But it was the tunnels he was having a hard time getting his head around, and the depths of evil he knew no one would ever believe.

"Every time I close my eyes, I see hell. How do you do this?" His head was swimming with so much, including so many unanswered questions. "What will happen to them?"

The bartender was now in back, but he still wasn't free to talk openly about anything, he remembered. Raven had reminded him they had a job to do. This was human trafficking, the dark and dirty that no one saw, crimes against humanity, against children. It was a military op, and military justice. That was all he knew. Yet he now understood that what he'd seen on his island only scratched the surface of a truly dark and ugly reality.

Baldy dragged his gaze away, taking in the room, everyone, everything. "You know, how I look at it is that someone needs to do this. I can tell you I wasn't always a good man, and I did things I never want my kids to know. You religious, Mark?"

What an odd question, considering what they were doing.

"Not particularly."

"At one time, I said the same thing—until my first day with this team. We found ourselves raiding a house at three a.m. in what I like to call the land of Oz, urban to the core, million-dollar townhomes with swimming pools. It was owned by the governor, and his wife was locked in a panic room with the kids. The fucker had hanged himself because he knew we were coming. In a back bedroom was a trap door that went down under the house to a cellar where he'd kept kids to satisfy his perversions.

"Because he wasn't that smart, he'd photographed everything, every child and every sick fucking thing he was into. It was in that moment I realized I couldn't live with myself if I allowed fuckers like that to live and hold the kind of power over you and me that they do. We are the good guys. We're rough around the edges, tarnished and banged up and grizzled. Sometimes we even find ourselves in the gutter. But we're angels, going in to rescue these innocents…"

"Angels? I'm no angel, not even close," Mark said. He finished off his beer and settled the bottle back on the bar when he felt Baldy tap his arm, leaning close to him.

"What do you believe, Mark, that angels never get their hands dirty, that they stay all nice and clean and shiny with halos, always smiling, and the darkness never touches them? No. That's us, and we're doing what few can or would do. Innocence is something evil preys on, something it needs to survive. If you'd told me this before I saw what I've seen, I wouldn't have believed it, but I do now. These are monsters who consume innocence. Predators are everywhere. They have agents, business managers, stock options, private islands, second and third homes. They dress well, talk well, and when they slip up, they just hire a marketing firm to polish their image."

Baldy kept his voice low, looking around, but it was just them leaning against the bar now. A jukebox was playing in the background, a song Mark wasn't even listening to. "Good is the only way to take out the bad, and these very bad people have done this for so long and been able to keep doing it. So many people work for them and will step in and do what they ask. Those tunnels, you saw the maps. They're everywhere. Which branch of the government do you think financed it and built it? Off the books, of course. Think about it. To create this takes technology, equipment, manpower, and years and years. Most in the military know about the tunnels, just not everything. Kind of sick to think this could be just below where you're living, underground, right beneath your feet, and you wouldn't even know."

Mark had both his hands on the bar now, his cell phone lying there. "Does it get worse?"

"It doesn't get better. The week before you came, we were down in South America. A school for girls had been sponsored and set up by a big-name celebrity. The news had said they were being given a future..." He shook his head. "Just not a future anyone would sign up for. There's a website, one of many, for a giant retailer that has listings for shoes. But just one shoe will be listed for several thousand dollars. The description will mention that there's only one left, size six, which is code for a six-year-old, and then to describe the product, they'll use terms like 'one dirty laundry footwear for a girl,' which means 'one Chinese girl.' These pedophiles know where to look. They understand the code. It may not seem like it, but we're making a difference. Look at what we went into, a lavish country estate that would be anyone's dream to own, yet horror lay underneath it. They're not all like this. Some are not as bad, some are worse. Some have just children, some women, some other things."

"I have a baby on the way," Mark said. "I don't know how to do this. How can I protect them?"

"Well, one, you call your wife and tell her you love her," Baldy said. "When you go home, you hug her, and you hug that kid when it's born. Don't let your heart get pulled into hate. Every person who did this or was part of it will have to answer to his or her maker. We put a bullet in how many down there? I guarantee you each one of them would have said, 'I was just doing my job.' Sure, two more may take their places tomorrow, but in three days we've cleared out a giant cancerous nest. It'll be blown up, and the news will report it as an earthquake. Sometimes it's just too deep to blow, so we flood it. Remember the flood on the west coast last year, the bridges that were washed out?" Baldy held up two fingers to the bartender at the end, who had reappeared, then looked back over to Mark. "Don't fester, or it'll eat you up. Call your wife."

"And tell her what? She knows me better than anyone. She'll know something is wrong, and I can't tell her any of it."

An odd smile pulled at Baldy's lips. Two beers appeared in front of them, and he reached for one and held it out to Mark.

"What will happen to Hughes?" Mark said. He'd seen the tech giant too many times on TV, the news, as part of some international forum.

"A swift military trial. He'll meet his maker. There's no coming back from what he did, but at the same time, someone like him has a lot of powerful people in his pocket, watching his back and making it so he can do all this. We'll try to find out their names. He may talk or he may not."

Mark lifted his beer, but he really didn't want it. "Will people ever know about all this, my family, my wife, the country? What about all the little ones? What happens to them?"

Baldy looked away. "They'll get the help they need, not in the system. The ones who can be saved will be. That's all I was told. Just think of the ones who'll live now, who never would've had a chance if we hadn't gone in. But no, you'll never see it on the news. These parasites own and control what you see, what you hear, what you know and believe. Maybe one day, and I pray it's not far off, the truth will come out in a way that can't be controlled.

"But think about what you saw, and ask yourself, would the average person, whose biggest challenge in a day is having to walk twelve blocks because he can't find a parking spot, or arguing with his spouse about whose turn it is to cook dinner, take out the trash, or walk the dog, or not getting an appointment to get her nails done, or having wine spilled all over his most expensive suit, do you really believe that person would want to know, let alone be able to handle, what you did and what you saw?"

Baldy held out his beer to Mark's and tapped the neck of the bottle with it. "Drink up and call your wife. But remember, too, that on every call you make, someone is listening." Then he pushed away from the bar and tapped Mark's shoulder.

Mark reached for his phone and took another swallow of his beer as he listened to the ring, then the click and her soft voice.

"Hello?"

"Hey, sorry I missed your call," he said. "Were you sleeping?" He heard rustling and pictured her in bed.

"It's fine. I'm glad you called. You okay? Haven't heard from you. Was starting to get worried."

Mark watched as the door to the bar opened and Mike Smith and Raven walked in. He didn't wave to them, just turned back to his beer, the phone to his ear. "Don't worry, I'm fine. Tell me about you, the baby. Is she kicking?"

"And what if it's a boy?"

"You know it doesn't matter to me. A healthy baby is all I want. I miss you. I love you."

There was silence on the other end. "The bed is lonely without you. Lucky and Sarge have both taken over your side."

"Well, tell them not to get too comfortable. Get some sleep. I'll try to call tomorrow."

"Mark?"

He hoped she wouldn't ask him what he'd done, what he'd seen. "Yeah?"

"You get some sleep, too. I love you," she said, and after she hung up, he put his cell phone down on the bar, glanced over his shoulder to the team he was part of, and willed for his family, his wife, to never know the things he'd seen.

Billy Jo had moved her seat back as far as she could and just barely reached the brake as she slowed her car on a narrow dirt driveway filled with deep ruts and overgrown brush. Ahead was a faded old green and white holiday trailer with a wooden deck and smoke rising from the chimney pipe of a woodstove. A light blue compact was parked off to the side, an older-model Honda that had duct tape around the left taillight reflector, and next to it was the sheriff's car, Raul leaning against it.

Billy Jo parked beside him, turned off the engine, and pressed the button to unfasten her seatbelt just as her door was pulled open. When he smiled, lines formed around his eyes from the sun and the weather, she figured. He shook his head, and she wondered whether he was trying not to laugh as he held out his hand to her. She bumped the steering wheel with her baby, which was almost ready to be born.

"Come on, I'll give you a hand," he said. "Man, you look as if you're about to drop that kid."

She set her hand in his after reaching for her bag, feeling the awkwardness as she slid one leg out and moved her seat back again. Raul helped her out and didn't let go of her hand as she took a step in one of the muddy ruts, wearing her baggy maternity sweats and a bulky sweater overtop because that was all that fit. He closed her door.

"You didn't have to come all the way out here," she said. "I can handle this myself, you know."

His gaze lingered on her, then fell to her baby. She had dropped her bag in the mud, and he said, "No, no, I'll get it. Just stay there. When are you due, anyways? Thought you'd have had the baby by now."

"I'll have you know my due date isn't for another week."

He made a face. "You heard from that husband of yours?"

What was she supposed to say? Mark called when he could. Raul was still holding her bag out to her, and she reached for it and slid it over her shoulder. "Four days ago," she replied. "Said it would likely be a few days before I heard from him again." She had to remind herself she wasn't needy, but she hadn't expected to miss him as much as she did. She wondered how much Raul knew, because he never asked.

"I'm sure he'll be in touch, but I'm just a phone call away if you need anything. Until he gets back," he said. He really was a great guy.

"You know Gail is staying with me," Billy Jo said, then heard the creak of the trailer door, and Raul looked away from her and did that thing of his that made her swear he saw everything.

He tapped her arm. "Gail tells me so every day," he

said before calling out, "Good morning, Ms. Palmer. How are you today?"

Damn, he really had that friendliness down in his drawl. He stood there beside her, resting his hands on his waist, leaning one foot forward. Billy Jo pulled at her fall coat, which was hanging open because she could no longer zip it up. In the doorway was Irene, her wavy hair tied back at the sides, with frizzy tendrils breaking free. Her sweater had a hole at the waist, and from where she stood, Billy Jo could see it was frayed at the wrists.

"As good as can be," Irene said. "Why're you here?"

Billy Jo didn't miss the edge in her voice, the distrust, as if she wanted to say, "What the hell do you want?" She pulled in a breath, which was becoming more of a challenge, feeling the baby's foot on her bladder and what felt like a fist pushing her ribs. "We have some news and wanted to see how you and Mila are doing."

The little girl appeared just behind Irene, sock footed, her round face pressed to her mother's leg, her hand gripping her navy sweatpants.

"What news?" It came out sharply. "Go on, back in," she said gently to Mila, then closed the door on the little girl after shooing her along.

Raul nodded. "You doing okay there, Irene?" he asked.

Irene had her arms pulled across her chest, and she nodded. "Just got a cord of wood delivered and was told you sent it over. I can't pay you for it."

Billy Jo turned to Raul, because this was the first she was hearing about it.

"You owe me nothing, Irene," he said. "Just helping out, is all. Was extra wood I cut up on the weekend, and

I didn't need it. Knew you could use it. The nights are getting colder."

Irene made a face and looked away. She was wearing old slippers on the deck. Billy Jo dragged her gaze from Raul to her and back. Irene nodded. "Thank you, then."

"Listen," he said. "I've got an old freezer that I have no use for. It can plug in there, sit on your deck. Holds a lot of meat. I hunt, always have. Took down a deer, and it's too much for me, so I'll bring some around once the butcher is done, fill up the freezer for you and the girl."

Billy Jo didn't have a clue what to say. She hadn't expected this, and she couldn't pull her gaze from Raul.

"Again, I can't pay you for it," Irene said.

"Where I come from, we don't take money," Raul said. "You doin' okay, you and the little one?"

Billy Jo felt something soften inside her, something she hadn't felt in a long time. This man was nothing like she'd expected.

Irene nodded. "We are, thank you."

Raul glanced down to Billy Jo. Maybe this was her cue, but what was she supposed to say? She'd basically hit roadblock after roadblock, and Raul had uncovered what she couldn't. "Billy Jo has been digging around about what happened to your daughter," he said. "There are people who care, Irene, to make things right." He was looking right at her again, waiting for her to talk. He really did have a way about him.

"The kidney that was taken from your daughter," Billy Jo said. "We've been looking into who did that to her. There were no records of why child services had her in the children's hospital or who ordered the kidney taken out, who signed off on it. But records were found from the Transplant Society and COTA. A bureaucrat passed a bill some time ago allowing guardians of child wards of the state to make decisions on all health-related issues, including organ donations. The man who signed the order allowing your daughter's kidney to be taken out and given for transplant, his name was Jonas Wilcox." She felt a hand on her arm and Raul's kind eyes on her.

He continued for her. "Your daughter's kidney was transplanted into a patient in Texas. Unfortunately, Mr. Wilcox is a supervisor in the Tacoma office, and no criminal charges can be filed against the doctors, the nurses, the hospital, or the social worker, as a legal bill was passed to allow this to happen. I'm sorry, Irene. I wish this never happened to your little girl."

Irene's face was tight, and she nodded. Billy Jo wondered if it was anger or sadness that made Irene nod, her lips tight, shaking her head.

"So they can just do what they want with my daughter," she said.

"No," Raul said. "I promise you, not as long as I'm here, and Billy Jo. We'll keep digging. If there's a way for you to get justice, I'll find it for you. You have my word."

Maybe it was the slow, deliberate way he spoke, or maybe it was the passion in him, but Billy Jo really believed everything he said deeply.

"You call me anytime," he continued, "to vent, to yell, or if you need anything. I mean it, Irene." He pulled out his card and held it out to her, and she hesitated only a second before taking it. Then she walked back to her tiny old trailer without another word, pulled open the door, and stepped inside. The door closed sharply behind her, and Billy Jo turned to the deputy who'd surprised her over and over.

"Why didn't you tell her it was a Texas billionaire who got her daughter's kidney or the fact that I discovered nothing at all?" she said. "It was you who found it out, and how I still don't know, considering all the brick walls I hit." She was facing him awkwardly, her hand on her baby, feeling so damn uncomfortable. "You really killed a deer, sent firewood… Who are you?"

He lifted his hand, motioning her to her car, and he pulled open her door for her. "Just a kid from the hills of Appalachia," he started.

Billy Jo rested her hand on the frame of the door. Pain had come out of nowhere. "Agh…" She winced and leaned in, fisting her hand. Tightness pulled across her belly. *Holy shit!* "No, not yet," she bit out, still wincing.

"What's wrong?" Raul said. "Are you okay? Billy Jo, are you in labor?"

She looked over to Raul, feeling the burn, thinking of what the midwife had said, that labor was uncomfortable. She was wrong on that; it hurt like hell. "Fuck, no! This can't be happening. Another week! The baby isn't supposed to be here for another week."

"Well, I hate to break this to you, darling, but babies come on their own time, when they're good and ready. Leave your car. I'll drive you to the hospital. Come on."

Billy Jo pulled in a breath, feeling the pain easing. She didn't move, still leaning against her car. "I'm not having my baby in a hospital. I have a midwife. I'm having it at home. Haven't even told Mark. I planned on it, but…" She gestured vaguely.

Raul took her bag, which had slipped off her shoulder. "Well, okay," he said. "We won't stand here, debating this. I'll drive you home. You call your midwife on the way. You want to call anyone else?" He'd already closed her door and was leading her, one hand on her arm, over to the sheriff's cruiser. He opened the passenger door to help her in, then set her bag at her feet.

"I need my phone," she said. "It's in my bag."

He lifted it and opened it for her, and she pulled out her cell phone, wishing Mark were there.

"I'll call Mark on the way," she said. Raul was still leaning in. The blue of his eyes was so different from Mark's, but they exuded something genuine from deep within. She realized she'd never met anyone like him. It was wisdom or something, an old soul.

"You're going to be fine," he said. "My mother had us all at home. There's nothing to it." Then he closed her door.

She went to call her midwife, but she dialed Mark first. It went right to voicemail, and she shut her eyes, hating the generic computer message. "Hey, Mark, it's Billy Jo. I'm in labor. Can you call me, please?"

Raul slid behind the wheel and gestured to her. "Put your seatbelt on," he said. "Don't worry. First babies, I've been told, can take a while."

CHAPTER

Sixteen

The hot shower welcomed Mark as he leaned one hand against the tile wall. The glass door was steamed up, and he wished for just a moment that he could forget the darkness that seemed to fill his days. He'd been forced to write out his memories in pen, the details never to be seen by anyone, maybe to give his brain a way to handle everything. What he had seen could break the strongest of men and women.

He heard a pounding at the door.

"I'm in the shower!" he yelled. "Leave me alone." He knew it had come out rather sharply, but he wasn't ready yet for what they had to do today or for conversation of any kind.

With a click of the lock, the door opened.

"What the fuck?" Mark said. "I'm in the shower!"

"Don't you answer your phone?" Mike said. "It's been blowing up, and now so's mine. Your wife's in labor."

A towel was tossed over the top of the shower door

as Mark turned off the water. He reached for it and wrapped it around his waist. "Billy Jo? Shit!" He stepped out of the shower, and Mike tossed him another towel, standing there in the doorway, the light from the hall spilling in.

"Yeah," he said. "Get dressed. Gopher has already called the pilot who'll pick you up at the lake. Be in the truck in five minutes."

Mark had already run the towel over his head and arms, reached for a clean charcoal sweater, and pulled it on. He flicked his gaze over to Mike, who was still in the doorway. "You going to watch me dress? Get out."

Mike lifted his hands and stepped out, letting the door close. Mark tossed the towel and pulled on faded blue jeans and socks, then shoved his feet in the combat boots he'd worn since he'd been there. He didn't bother lacing them before yanking open the door and running two doors down to the room he shared with Baldy.

Inside, on the steel table beside his small single bed, were his pen and journal, his phone on top. He yanked open the small closet and pulled out his dark coat, then shrugged it on before grabbing his phone and shoving it in his pocket. He was out the door and running down the hall, passing three of the guys.

"Hey, newbie, where's the fire?" Dion called out.

"My wife's having the baby!" he yelled without turning back.

Behind him, the guys shouted out congratulations, as well as orders to get moving and a few other things he didn't pay much mind to. He was out the locked interior door, seeing the same guy at the security desk, and Mike was pushing the front door open now and gesturing to him, saying, "Hurry up!"

Outside, in whiteout conditions from an overnight snow, a truck was idling.

"Let's go, let's go," Mike said, heading down the concrete steps, which needed to be shoveled again. He pulled open the passenger door at the same time Mark pulled open the back, and the truck was already moving before he closed it. Gopher was behind the wheel, a dark knit cap over his head. Mark's breath fogged from the cold and the fact that the truck was barely warm.

"Who called you?" Mark said as he pulled out his phone and dialed his voicemail.

"Spoke with a Gail," Mike said. "Guess they gave up when you didn't answer. I know your wife's at home right now. Someone will pick you up as soon as you land."

Mark was listening to Billy Jo's first message: "I'm in labor. Can you call me, please?" He deleted it and went on to the next: "Where are you? Why haven't you called me back? I wasn't supposed to do this alone…" Okay, now she sounded pissed. He went to the third message: "Mark, this is Gail. This is the real deal!" He hit delete and was already dialing Billy Jo's number. It rang once, twice as the truck slid sideways and was righted.

"Ah, hello?"

He would have known Gail's voice anywhere. "Gail, it's Mark. I just got your message. Billy Jo's really in labor? I'm on my way." He thought he heard something in the background, a rustling, voices.

"How far away are you?" Gail said. "Here, Billy Jo wants to talk to you." Then she was gone, and he heard rustling again, her saying something.

"Mark, I'm sorry, I'm in labor," Billy Jo said. "I'm at

home." She stopped talking, and he was sure he heard her yelling.

"Mark, this is Gail again."

"Why is she at home?" Mark said. "Go to the hospital. I'll meet you there. I'm just catching a float plane. Will be landing in…" He let the phone slip away.

Mike was in the front, looking back to him. "About an hour and a half, thereabouts."

Mark slid the phone back to his ear. "An hour and a half," he said. "What did the doctor say?"

He felt so damn helpless. He could hear Billy Jo yelling in the background, and he wanted to kick himself for being so wrapped up in himself that he'd missed her call. He could've already been back there.

"She's having the baby at home," Gail said. "Guess she didn't tell you."

Mark wasn't sure he'd heard right.

"Billy Jo wants to talk to you again," Gail said. "Her labor is really progressing. The midwife is here."

Mark said nothing.

Billy Jo came back on the phone. "Can you hurry, please? I just don't want to have our baby in the hospital. I meant to tell you. I'm sorry. I have a midwife, but dammit, Mark…"

He heard her yelling, and he winced. He'd known labour was bad, but he was hearing the reality and feeling so damn helpless this far away.

"Okay, she told you, and now you know." It was Gail back on the line. "So hurry up and get back here, because the last thing I want is for you to miss the birth of your first baby. Carmen will pick you up. Call her from the air."

He made himself pull in a breath. "I'll do my best. Can you give the phone back to Billy Jo, please?"

"Sure, just a second." He wondered if Gail had stepped out of the room. He heard her say, "Mark wants to talk to you."

"Hey, babe," he said. "I want you to hang in there. Try to hold out until I get there. And this midwife thing isn't a big deal. You should have told me—because I've got to tell you, I think you made the right choice. I love you." He heard her breathe, and then she sniffed. He thought she was crying. "Hey, babe, I'm on my way. I'm not going to miss this."

"You'd better not," she said. "I love you."

Yeah, she was crying. Then she hung up, and Mark took in Mike watching him in the rear-view mirror. He hesitated before shoving his phone in his pocket and then running both his hands over his face.

"Hey there, newbie, she's going to be fine," Mike said. "Women have been having babies since the beginning of time."

Mark glanced out the side window, which was still frosted up. "She's having the baby at home with a midwife. I think she didn't want to tell me because she thought I'd fight her on it. But I'm so damn relieved…"

Mike reached back and patted his shoulder. "Things often work out in ways we never expect. You call us as soon as she has the baby. Let us know. There it is." He pointed through the windshield to the lake ahead, where a float plane hung in the sky, just about to land.

As Gopher pulled into the lot by the dock, Mike looked back to Mark. The two stepped out as soon as the truck was parked, and Mike held out Mark's cell phone, the one that had been taken from him.

"Mark, each of us knows when we're done what we have to do here," he said. "You go and be with your wife and that baby." Mark thought Mike was about to say something else, but he only shook his head and gestured to the float plane, which was now docked. "Run," he said. "Go be with your wife, and congratulations."

****

Carmen had dropped him off after waiting for him at the dock. She'd even flashed her lights a few times to get him home in under ten minutes, and as soon as he walked through the front door, he heard yelling. The dogs barked and came running, Lucky first, then Sarge, tails wagging.

"Hey, there, missed you," he said, then ran his hand quickly over the two dogs and pushed past them as he strode down the hall.

"Damn, Mark, where are you?" Billy Jo called out.

Gail stood just inside his bedroom, her arms crossed, with a smile just for him. His wife was leaning over the side of the bed, resting on her forearms. As she turned her head, looking right at him, he could see the pain she was in. Her forehead and brow were damp, her cheeks pink. A woman with a round face and dark hair was rubbing her back. Billy Jo had her heavy socks on and just a nightshirt.

The dogs were right there, bumping Mark and whining. "Hey, you two, out," he ordered, then headed for Billy Jo. "I missed you too," he said as he ran his hand over her back and leaned down to kiss her cheek. "I'm here. What do you need?"

She groaned again and put her forehead to the bed

as he ran his hands over her shoulders, her back, looking over to who he figured was the midwife. He stood and shrugged out of his coat, giving it a toss to the easy chair in the corner. Gail was herding the dogs out of the bedroom.

"I'm Mark, the husband," he said. "You're the midwife?"

"She knows who the fuck you are, Mark," Billy Jo snapped. She was groaning again. Mark rested his hand on her back.

"Nice to meet you, Mark. I'm Deborah. I think you just made it in time. Your wife was fighting it and refusing to deliver this baby until you got here. Come on, Billy Jo. I think you're almost there. Mark, help Billy Jo back on the bed. I'll get you to hold her up from behind."

"Oh, Mark, it hurts."

He had her standing and managed to get her on the bed. The duvet was gone, replaced by a cover like he'd seen in hospitals. He sat behind her, letting her lean against him, and the midwife was in front of her, sitting on the edge of the bed.

"Come on, Billy Jo, knees up," she said.

Mark held his wife, taking in the moment. He kissed her cheek, and she reached for his hand to hold on. The midwife looked up to him and Billy Jo with a smile.

"And you're ready," she said. "On the next contraction, Billy Jo, you're going to push."

Mark had never in his life seen anything so perfect. The tiny face peered up at him, wrapped in a soft white blanket. The mouth, he swore, was all Billy Jo. She was so tiny, fitting in the crook of his arm, so fragile, so innocent. As she stared up at him, her eyes open, he knew she needed him to defend her, to protect her from everything.

"You counted all her fingers and toes?" Billy Jo was propped up in bed on her side with a blanket over her, and damn, she looked so beautiful.

"Look at her mouth," he said. "I swear she's going to have your personality. She's perfect." Mark leaned down with the baby cradled in his arm, his other around Billy Jo, and he pressed a kiss to her lips. "How're you doing?" he said as he pulled back.

She reached up and touched his face, the beard he'd started growing a few weeks earlier, then rested her hand on their baby. "Better now that you're here," she said. "I didn't think you'd make it. It was hard, Mark. I know I said I was okay with you going and doing what you needed to do, but I really missed you. Not sure about the beard, though." She made a face and yawned.

"I'll shave it off."

She ran her hands over it again and shook her head. "No, it might grow on me. I'm sorry I didn't tell you about the midwife. I was planning on it, and then you were pulled away, and I just didn't want to tell you over the phone. Are you mad?"

What was he supposed to say, considering what he'd seen?

"No, I'm actually relieved," he said. "Why didn't you want to tell me? You thought I wouldn't be okay with it?"

She shrugged and licked her lips. "It was silly. I just didn't want to do what everyone expected. Why does it seem everyone has her baby in a hospital? I looked into it, and it seems so much changed after the Second World War, people's way of doing everything. I saw my regular MD, and when he gave me all the pamphlets, the maternity ward information, I had the feeling he would basically just show up to deliver the baby. He spoke of complications, saying sometimes it's better for the mom to have a C-section. So I did some digging, and I found Deborah, called her, and met with her. In our first appointment, I was surprised how much more she knew. There are too many things with the hospital and the system that I just don't trust anymore, Mark, not after what we've seen."

He let his gaze linger, seeing how tired she was. "It was a good call, but you still should have told me."

She nodded. "When do you have to leave?"

He couldn't look away from his daughter, terrified of

everything that could happen to her. "I'm not going back, Billy Jo. I'm done. I did what I needed to do."

She frowned. Maybe he'd surprised even himself a little, but there wasn't a chance he could walk away and leave his newborn baby girl and his wife unprotected. He was feeling so many things, including a fear that had come out of nowhere at the memory of the children he'd tried to save.

"What about the kids, what you were doing?" Billy Jo said. "I have an idea, Mark, and I know how important it is…"

"But so are you," he said, not letting her finish. "Family first. You're right, it was important, but someone told me you know when you're done."

She said nothing, not looking away from him. Then she did. "We haven't talked about names."

He couldn't pull his gaze from his daughter, and he wondered for a moment if this was what his parents had felt for him. This kind of love was bigger than anything, a bond he knew was impossible to break. "How about Grace?" He flicked his gaze over to Billy Jo, feeling the warmth of his daughter and how content she was. He didn't want to let her go. His wife was thinking, he knew, from the way she frowned. Maybe she'd say no.

"I like it," she said. There was a tap on the open door, and Mark looked up to see the midwife leaning in.

"Hey, you two, let me just have a look at that precious little girl. You pick a name yet?" The midwife stepped in and walked around the bed, and Mark stood up.

He hesitated a second, looking to Billy Jo, who nodded to him. "This is Grace," he said. "Grace

Friessen." He let the midwife take the baby, and she lowered her to the bed.

"I promise I'll give her right back, Dad," Deborah said.

Mark glanced over to Billy Jo. "I need to make some calls. I'll be back soon," he said. He walked around the bed, taking another look at a miracle he wondered what good he'd done to deserve. Then he strode over to the chair and reached for his coat. He took in Gail leaning in the doorway, smiling brightly at him.

"Congratulations, Dad." She tapped his arm, and he stopped beside her and kissed her cheek.

"Thanks, Gail," he said before heading into the kitchen. The dogs were in the living room, curled up together in their dog bed, and Harley, Billy Jo's cat, was sleeping on the back of the sofa. He pulled both cell phones from his pocket, his old one and his new one, but when he powered on the new one, it was no longer in service.

He reached for his old cell phone and turned it on to see a text from Mike Smith, a number. He dialed and heard a click.

"So tell me, boy or girl?" It hadn't even rung.

"Girl," Mark said. "I'm not coming back." He walked over to the sliding glass door. Outside, darkness was settling in.

"When you're done, you're done," Mike said. "It was a pleasure, Mark. You made a difference."

Mark shook his head, thinking of the journal he'd started. "I left my things."

"I'll have them sent to you. Take care of that wife and baby."

He hadn't thought it would be this easy. "You knew I

wasn't coming back, didn't you?" Mark said. He wasn't sure what he heard in the background. Then he thought a door closed.

"I'm good at reading people, and you served your purpose, Mark," Mike said.

"I don't feel like I did enough." He wondered if he'd always feel this way.

"Listen to me: Half our fight is waking people up, and not just everyday people. The objective, really, is to wake up every sheriff in this country. Because once your eyes are open, you're not going back to sleep. You know what to look out for, and I'll see to it that you know how to get a hold of me. You take care of that wife, that baby, and you take care of your people on that island."

Then Mike hung up.

Mark listened to the soft cry of his baby girl, Grace, and his wife's laughter. He thought of the moment nearly two years earlier when he'd first set foot on the island. He'd already figured out so much about the world and how it worked, but now he realized he'd really known nothing at all.

"It's good to have you back, Chief," Lacy said as she set a mug of coffee on Mark's desk, which he stood behind. "How're mom and baby?"

Mark was still thinking of his wife and Grace, who'd both been tucked in, sound asleep, when he left.

"You get much sleep?" Lacy continued.

Mark yawned as he shrugged out of his black down coat and tossed it over the coat tree. He gave his head a shake before reaching for the black coffee, taking in the dogs, whom Lacy had just put more kibble out for. "Sleep?" he said. "A few hours, here and there. Then I have a moment where I think, 'Holy God, I'm responsible for this tiny thing.' I wonder if that ever goes away. It seemed she woke every two hours last night. But they're both good, both sleeping when I left. We named her Grace."

Mark had even changed her and held her, and Billy Jo had nursed her. He was still in awe of the miracle. He pulled his cell phone from his pocket and took in the photo he snapped the night before of Billy Jo holding

Grace. It was the same one he'd sent to his parents and to hers, Chase and Rose McCabe.

Lacy took his phone. "Ah, Mark, she's beautiful. She has your red hair, I see." She smiled brightly, handing the phone back.

"Yup, she'll be a redhead, but with her mother's personality, I think." He took in the image of his wife and daughter again, then put his cell phone down. "Talked to our parents last night. Of course, they all want to come out and see the baby. Well, I think it's more my mom and Rose who can't wait to get their hands on her, hold her, spoil her. Gail was up when I left, too, and I know she's more than happy to help."

When Grace had woken the last time at six a.m., Gail had been in the kitchen, making coffee. That was the only reason he was there now.

"Well, I won't invade you, but I've picked up something for the baby," Lacy said. "I'll give you a few days and then drop by so I can see her, have my turn holding her."

He took in the quiet station and the clock on the wall. It was just after seven a.m., but then, Lacy was always there before anyone. "So how did it go while I was gone? Any problems, anything I should know about? My desk has never looked so neat." There wasn't a file anywhere. The desk appeared dusted, and even the pens were neatly tucked in a plastic holder on the side.

Lacy was in blue jeans and a light long-sleeved shirt, her graying hair pulled back in a ponytail. She crossed her arms over her chest. "Better than expected. That Raul Booth, he's a keeper, Mark, a fine human being. He's got that quality that comes from deep within. You don't often see it, but I knew the moment I met him. He made everything here easier. Where'd you find him, anyway?"

Behind her, the door opened, and she turned. Mark took in a man with dark hair and a well-tended beard, average build and height, in a dark coat and blue jeans.

"Good morning, Raul," Lacy called out. "Was just talking about you with the chief. Come in and meet him."

"Good morning to you, Lacy," Raul said. "You made coffee again? Thank you. It's a welcome thing every morning I walk in."

Mark hadn't expected the drawl or the kindness. Raul stopped in front of Lacy with a smile, and her face lit up in return. He dragged his gaze over to Mark.

"Chief Friessen, it's a pleasure to meet you," he said. "How's your wife doing? Heard you had a daughter."

"I'll pour you a coffee," Lacy said to him, and he nodded with a smile that seemed to radiate from him.

"That is mighty kind," he said. "Thank you, Lacy. I surely appreciate everything you do here." Then he was looking back over to Mark. He stepped into the office fully, his heavy brown coat unzipped, showing a dusty blue shirt underneath.

"Billy Jo is good," Mark said. "We named her Grace. I guess I owe you a debt for looking out for her. Gail told me everything you did."

Raul was already shaking his head. Then Lacy walked in, saying, "Here's your coffee, Raul. Cream, just the way you like it."

"Lacy, you're a gem. Thank you," Raul said. Then Lacy was gone, and Raul closed the door and took a swallow of coffee, making a sound of appreciation. "You have some really good people here, Chief."

Mark didn't pull his gaze, taking in a man who appeared not much older than he, with weather-etched lines around his soft brown eyes, so much like his dad. Then Raul pulled a badge from his pocket, the deputy badge that had once belonged to Carmen, and placed it on the desk along with keys to the sheriff's cruiser.

"What's this?" Mark said.

Raul was already nodding. "I was here to help out. A favor was asked. You're back now, Chief. Time for me to move on."

Mark took in the badge and the man. "Would like it if you'd stay. The position is yours."

Raul was already shaking his head. "I appreciate the offer, Chief. This is a mighty fine community, and you're a lucky man, with what you have here, but you don't need me here now."

Mark nodded. "How do you know Mike Smith?"

Raul said nothing. He glanced away and up at the ceiling, which gave Mark the sense someone was listening in. It had come out of nowhere. He wondered if that was what Raul was alluding to. "You know, where I come from, we have friends for life. Mike was a towny, and I was a kid in the hills with hand-me-down shoes my mother patched and clothes that were either too big or too short."

"You were friends, then, growing up?"

Raul shook his head, and an odd smile twisted his lips. "No, the opposite. Hated the prick. He was one of a gang of losers who mercilessly teased and taunted my family with cruel words. Always dressed nice and never let an opportunity to grind me down go wasted. He let me know who his father was, how I'd never amount to anything. But growing up, I wanted something different.

I knew my options were bleak, so I walked into an Army recruitment office and was offered a ten thousand signing bonus and all kinds of benefits. Next I knew, I was enlisted.

"I found myself sent over to Afghanistan and in the back of a military truck, on the way to a base, when the truck in front was hit by artillery. A shitshow. Next, I'm being dragged by the back of my uniform. Didn't have a clue who rescued me, but he came by medical after I was stitched up. A bullet had grazed me. He introduced himself, as if I could've ever forgotten who he was, and he apologized for being a shit when we were kids. He'd more than made up for it, saving my ass. He was on some special assignment and just happened to be there at the right time. I finished out my three-year enlistment and went back home, and then one day he's on my doorstep asking for my help."

Raul looked away, and Mark couldn't shake the feeling that Raul understood what he'd done, what he'd seen. "I've been where you are," he continued. "Mike saved my ass more times than I can count. I know what you've seen. I know what you now carry. It really makes you see the world a different way, be more appreciative of the good things. You did your time, and now it's someone else's turn. You wake up enough like yourself, and that's how we bring this down." He was nodding, and the way he spoke, it was as if he were choosing his words carefully.

"How long were you with the team?"

There it was, a sad smile that pulled at the corners of his lips. "From the beginning. Eighteen months. It takes a piece out of you that you never get back. Mike is steady as they come, but he knew I was done before I did. So when he calls, says I'm needed, I go. I'm not needed here anymore, but I am somewhere else." He took another swallow of his coffee, then rested the mug on the edge of the desk beside his badge and keys. His hand lingered there a second before he reached out across the desk.

Mark shook it, feeling the firm grip and unwavering gaze.

"You take care of your baby girl," Raul said. "And tell your wife I said goodbye. She's a spitfire with a heart of gold and an unwavering moral compass. You're a lucky man." He reached into his pocket and pulled out a piece of paper, holding it in two fingers out to Mark.

"What is this?" Mark took the paper and opened it, seeing three names he didn't know handwritten in black ink.

"Where I come from, when a man puts his hands on another man's pregnant wife, there are consequences. The first two names are the hospital security guards who handcuffed your wife, which was how I first met her. Carmen sent them off with their tails tucked."

Mark just stared for a moment, feeling that burn of fire that would have him lighting someone's ass. "Excuse me, you're kidding, right? They handcuffed my pregnant wife? Why, where, what the fuck?"

Raul was not smiling. "Wouldn't kid about something like that. Didn't think it was my place to decide what happened, but it is yours. Out of this job, off the island…" He only shrugged, then nodded at the list. "The last name is the Texas billionaire who received Mila Palmer's kidney, paid through an organ broker, funneled through COTA. You have to really dig in the paperwork, because on the surface, no one would question it. If you have enough money, you can buy anything."

"What am I supposed to do with this? JW Wall…?"

"Nothing," Raul said. "Just wanted you to know the name. You may be hearing some news about him in the coming days, is all. Again, Chief…"

"It's Mark." He cut him off, this man he realized had been sent to watch over his family, his community.

"Mark, it really was a pleasure." Then Raul turned and put his hand on the knob to pull it open.

"Raul, thank you for everything. You ever need anything, you call me—and I mean anything."

Raul nodded, pulling open the door, and strode out. Sarge walked over to him, tail wagging, and he leaned down and ran his hand over the pup, then said something to Lacy before hugging her and walking over to Carmen's empty desk. He pulled an envelope from his jacket pocket and set it on her desk, and as he was walking out the door, Carmen was coming in.

Mark didn't know what passed between them, but he heard him say, "I left you something on your desk." Then he was gone, and Mark only nodded to Carmen as she walked over to her desk and picked up an envelope with her name written on it.

"I can't believe he's leaving," she said. She opened the envelope and pulled out a card. "Damn, he's thoughtful," was all she said before looking away, sliding the card back in the envelope, and tucking it in her top drawer.

"Carmen, you want to take a ride?" Mark said.

She gave her head a shake before looking over to him. "Sure, where?"

"To the hospital, to have a word with those two clowns who put my wife in cuffs."

Carmen seemed to still, then slowly dragged her gaze over to him. "Billy Jo made me promise not to tell you."

He was already walking back to his office. "Oh, I would expect no less from her," was all he said. He reached for his coat and tucked the list of names in his jacket pocket along with his cell phone.

Carmen appeared in the doorway. "And what are we doing after having a word, exactly?"

"I'll figure that part out when we get there, but suffice it to say that neither of those clowns will ever work a job that gives them that kind of power again," Mark said. He reached for the badge Raul had left on his desk and tucked it in his drawer before tossing the cruiser keys to Carmen, who caught them with one hand.

"You drive," he said. "And one more thing, Carmen."

She didn't smile, and her brow furrowed.

"Thank you," he said.

She appeared confused. "For what?"

"For holding down the fort. For everything."

Gail was holding the baby, and Billy Jo had put her feet up on a stool where she sat in the easy chair in sweats and thick socks. When Mark walked out of the bedroom, she took in his face, which was now clean shaven.

"You shaved off the beard," she said.

He walked over to her and leaned down, and she slid her hand over the smoothness of his cheek before he kissed her and pulled away, then walked over to Gail and took the baby from her. "Just wanted a clean start," he said. "Man, she's beautiful."

The way he looked at their daughter, Billy Jo just knew he'd never let anything happen to her.

"So," Gail said, "I just heard from Carmen that you paid a visit to two security guards at the hospital."

Billy Jo frowned, and Mark let those amazing blue eyes settle on her.

"I met Raul Booth this morning," he explained. "He turned in his badge and left. Good man. He wanted me to pass along his goodbye to my spitfire of a wife. Then he gave me the names of the two security guards who decided to flex their muscles and cuff her. Yes, Billy Jo, I'm well aware you didn't want me to know, but you are my wife, and no one puts their hands on you. Had a word with the hospital administrator, who called in the two boys after I made it clear how I feel about someone playing cop. Of course, I was assured it would never happen again, and I said to all three of them that I knew without a doubt it would never happen again, because they knew what a mistake they'd made with the chief's wife, but that didn't mean they wouldn't do it to someone else's pregnant wife. Suffice it say, they've been relieved of their duties, and as long as I have a say, they will never work in security again. The hospital has been put on notice by me that no overreach will be tolerated."

Billy Jo didn't know what to say. She wondered if she'd ever get used to the way her husband had her back. "I'm sorry to see Raul leave."

Gail was smiling at the baby. "I heard he made a point of helping out the single mothers on the island, not just Irene Palmer but a few others who were struggling. Filled their freezers with fish and deer, chopped and split wood for a few. Can't say anyone has ever done that here."

Billy Jo suspected Raul was the kind of man who left every place he'd been just a little better. Just as she thought so, her phone dinged beside her on the end table, and she picked up her cell phone to see a text from him: *Dear Billy Jo, congratulations on your baby girl, Grace. Remember, justice is coming for the bad guys. Share this link with your husband. And until we meet again in another lifetime, all the best. Raul.*

"What is it?" Mark asked.

She followed the link and took in a news article. "A text from Raul, a link to a news article about a JW Wall in Texas who's been arrested for his involvement in the black-market purchase of a kidney, him and a broker who procures illegal organs for the highest bidder…" She held her phone out.

Mark walked over and took it with one hand, holding Grace in the other. An odd smile pulled at his lips. "Well, just maybe there's some justice after all," he said. Then Grace started fussing, and Mark walked her over and slid her into Billy Jo's arms. He ran his hand over her cheek and said, "It's going to be okay."

He didn't say anything else, but from the way his blue eyes lingered, the light that filled them, she realized he was right. Whatever darkness has settled on the island, she had a feeling it no longer had the hold it once had.

"I know it is," she said, then looked down to their baby girl. "We got this."

Mark knelt down, putting his hand over hers, over their baby. "Yeah," he said, "we got this."

Turn the page for a sneak peek of
THE HUNTED the newest release in *THE O'CONNELLS*
Available in print, eBook & audio

The Hunted

THE O'CONNELLS

When two prisoners escape and one is found dead, Marcus O'Connell finds himself being hunted—and the hunter could be someone he trusts.

One late night, Sheriff Marcus O'Connell receives a call about two escaped prisoners considered a danger to the community. A search is underway, and the warden has reason to believe the escaped convicts are headed toward Livingston. An urgent warning is issued: Shoot to kill.

Hours later, Marcus is called to a crime scene. The body of one of the escaped prisoners has been discovered deep in the woods, and the scene has already been lit up, with three prison guards standing over the body, along with the sheriff and deputy from the county over and a tracker with his dogs. A story has been neatly put together, and the group at the scene tries to send Marcus on his way.

Yet one prisoner is still missing. Marcus is told no investigation is necessary, that he should sign off on the case and walk away. But nothing adds up. The problem is that dead men can't talk, and Marcus can't shake the feeling that the story he's being told is a coverup for something far more sinister.

The Hunted

CHAPTER 1

T he sound of crickets punctuated the quiet neighborhood. Darkness had settled in, but Marcus needed a minute, as he leaned against the large porch beam, before he could lock up for the night and feel that all was okay in his part of the world. He lifted his hand in a wave to his brother Owen and his wife, Tessa, as they drove away in her small compact. Again, he took in the neighbors' houses. Next door, the lights were off and all seemed quiet.

Ryan and Jenny were already inside their house across the road, and the outside light was now off. Marcus waited for that feeling he got every night before locking up, an assurance that it would be okay for him to lay his head down and go to sleep. He counted heads, making sure everyone was okay, listening to the sounds inside his house, the fussing of Cameron, who was doing his nightly protest against going to sleep.

The screen door squeaked open behind him, and Marcus turned to see his dad step out, wearing blue jeans and a black t-shirt. He heard his mom and Reine talking inside. His dad nodded to him and headed over.

"Your mom is finishing up in the kitchen with Reine and Eva," Raymond said. "That boy of yours is just like you. You always fought your mom and argued every night about how you weren't tired, but a second later you'd be out cold. You didn't know how to stop."

Marcus turned to look back at the street. He was still trying to understand his dad. He leaned against the post on the porch, breathing in the warm summer night. The smell told him tomorrow would be another hot day.

"You were rather quiet tonight," Raymond said. "Everything okay?"

What was he supposed to say? This feeling had come out of nowhere. He couldn't remember ever having felt so unsettled, and he didn't have a clue what had caused it—family, life, something else?

"Just one of those days, you know," Marcus said, unable to find words to explain it.

His dad only nodded. It wasn't lost on Marcus that his dad had been forced to stick around Livingston because his mom had refused to leave her children and grandkids. His dad had a way of seeing everything. Marcus had figured that much out, but a stranger wouldn't have been able to tell, as Raymond never let his gaze linger too long.

Now he did, narrowing his eyes, peering out into the darkness. The stars were out, and a few streetlights were on. "Always the sheriff, looking out to make sure everyone is tucked in, safe," he said. "Expecting trouble?"

Marcus looked over to his dad. Inside, the house phone was ringing, and a second later, it was answered.

"You know something I don't?" he said. The sarcasm dripped.

His dad only shrugged. Marcus heard footsteps and pushed away from the post just as the screen door squeaked again, and Reine stepped out, her dark hair pulled back, wearing a peach sundress, barefoot.

"Marcus, it's for you," she said. "It's Therese." She held out the cordless phone.

Marcus didn't look over to his dad, who he knew was watching him in the way only Raymond O'Connell could. Marcus took the portable phone. "Thanks, Reine," he said, then waited as she walked back in the house. He put the phone to his ear, glancing only once to his dad, knowing his deputy called only if there was something he needed to handle. "What's up, Therese?"

"Sorry to call so late, Sheriff, but I have a message from the warden from Montana State. Two prisoners have escaped, and all he said was that they could be headed this way. I was about to call him back..." There was static on the line. His deputy was cutting in and out, as if she were driving.

"Hey, Therese, you're cutting out. You said two prisoners escaped from Montana State?" He was already walking back into the house and taking the stairs two at a time. Upstairs, Charlotte was reading to his son, whom he thought he heard jumping on his bed. Marcus was in his bedroom now, yanking open the closet door and opening the gun safe to retrieve his .357 SIG.

"Sorry, Sheriff," Therese said. "I'm about twenty minutes away, and the cell service is like shit out here. Picked up the message on the way. All it said was that two prisoners escaped. The warden is..."

"Kellogg," Marcus cut in, fastening the holstered

gun to the waistband of his jeans. As he closed up the gun safe, he pictured a man he'd met only a few times.

"I missed that part of the message," Therese said. "I'll give him a call and let you know what he says."

Marcus glanced to the open door. His wife now stood in the doorway. "No, Therese, I've got it," he said. "I'll have Charlotte check the message, and I'll give the warden a call."

She said nothing, and he noted her hesitation.

"Anything else?" he said, realizing it had come out rather short.

"No, that was all," Therese said. "You sure, Sheriff? I don't mind making the call. It may be nothing."

"Or it may be a lot," he said. "No, I've got this one." Then he hung up and held the phone out to Charlotte, taking in her wide eyes.

"What's going on, Marcus?"

He reached for his badge. "Prison break or something along those lines. Therese just called, said the warden at Montana State left a message. Two prisoners. I need you to get his number and play that message for me."

She was already nodding and dialing the office. Something about his wife handling phones and dispatching again settled him in ways he couldn't explain. She scribbled down the number on a pad of paper on the dresser just as his two-year-old son came running in, all smiles, appearing nowhere near ready to go to sleep.

Marcus reached for him and gave him a toss in the air, then held him and kissed his cheek. "Hey, you. Giving your mom a hard time? You're supposed to be asleep."

"Not tired."

"Yeah, well, you will be soon. Go get a book and get in bed."

"Here, Marcus, the number," Charlotte said. "The message is kind of garbled, but yes, it's something about two prisoners escaping."

He put Cameron down after kissing him again and reached for the paper and the phone, shaking his head over his rambunctious son.

Charlotte shook her head. "He's going to be the end of me. You know he argues every night about how he isn't tired?" She pulled her arms over her faded green t-shirt, her dark hair pulled up in a ponytail. "You're heading out, aren't you?"

"Yeah, after I call the warden," he said. "I don't like this."

There it was, that smile of hers he loved. She leaned in the doorway, glancing once over her shoulder down the hall to where their son's bedroom was as he dialed the phone.

"Montana State, warden's office." The voice was muffled, and Marcus had to really listen past the rough twang.

"This is Sheriff O'Connell, from Livingston. Is the warden there? I've got a message from him about a prison escape."

He heard a rustle on the other end, then a clunk. Evidently, whoever had answered barely knew how to use a phone. "Yeah, yeah," the person said, then yelled out, "Warden! Call for you from that Sheriff O'Connell."

Marcus reached for his wallet and stuffed it in his back pocket, then reached for his duty belt. Charlotte didn't look away, gesturing for an explanation, but Marcus only shook his head. There was another rustle on the phone.

"Sheriff? Warden Kellogg here." The man had a deep voice. "Afraid two prisoners escaped. Was discovered only a short time ago by one of the guards. We're in lockdown now. Just finished a count and are interrogating some prisoners. We know two got out for sure, but how, we have no idea. They likely had help from inside. I suspect they could be headed your way. These men are dangerous, both of them. I've already contacted state officials, as well, along with the other sheriffs in the area. An order has already been issued: Shoot to kill."

Marcus angled his head, looking right at Charlotte. He wasn't sure he'd heard the warden correctly. "You can't be serious," he said. "Who authorized that order? With all due respect, Warden, capturing the prisoners is the first priority."

"Sheriff O'Connell, these prisoners are a danger to the community," the warden said. "They will slit your throat and kill you without a second thought. If you want to dance around them and be the nice guy, do it on your own time and not at the detriment of the good people of Montana. You see them, you shoot them, because these two will do anything and everything to avoid capture. Killing, maiming, looting, burning. You want the details of what they'd do to your wife and sisters, everyone in your family, everyone you care about? If you want to argue with me about bringing them in alive, you can do it, but I don't want these two getting anywhere near innocent people. I've already reached out to Judge Harris, and photos of the prisoners have been sent to you."

Marcus didn't have a clue who these two prisoners were or what they'd done, but that sick feeling was back in his stomach with the image of the horror the warden had painted. Damn, what kind of evil had the two men done?

On the other end, the warden was talking to someone else. Then he addressed Marcus again. "Anything else, Sheriff? If not, I suggest you get your ass out there and start looking. Stan has faxed over the photos, and emails have gone out statewide."

Something about Warden Kellogg had always unsettled Marcus, but he couldn't put his finger on what it was. "Yeah, you said they could be headed my way. Why is that? They have family, friends, contacts here? I need all that information."

"Everything about both prisoners has been sent to you. One has a girlfriend, I understand, outside Livingston, and a brother up toward Billings. If that's all, Sheriff, I've got a fucking mess to handle here. You have any questions, get in touch with Sheriff Lester up in Stillwater County. He's got more on them, and he's been on this since word went out. And, Sheriff O'Connell? A word of advice. I understand you may want to give these men a second chance, but sometimes we're all better off if a criminal is six feet under. You understand?"

Yeah, he understood, but a knot twisted in his stomach as he looked over to his wife. He wondered if this explained the sick feeling he had or the cold sweat that had broken out up his spine. "Understood," he said.

"I'll start looking." Then he hung up and tossed the phone on the bed.

"What is it, Marcus?"

Marcus counted the extra clips in his duty belt, then walked over to his wife and ran his hand over her shoulder. "Warden says the prisoners had help from the inside to get out. Says they're dangerous. Photos have been faxed and emailed. Can you access those? I'm going to ask Mom and Dad to stay until I get back," he said. It was just a feeling he had, the need to keep his family together. "See if you can pull up the prisoners' files, too. Warden said they've been sent. I want to know everything about them: who they are, what they did, and exactly how dangerous they are."

He hurried down the stairs, and Charlotte was right behind him. Raymond was back in the house, and he could hear his mom, Reine, and Eva in the kitchen. Marcus stepped off the bottom step, and Charlotte moved around him into the living room, over to the small desk where her laptop was.

"What's going on?" Raymond said as Marcus reached for his sheriff's jacket and lifted it from the hook.

"Marcus, I just sent the photos and files to your phone," Charlotte called out.

Marcus pulled his iPhone from his coat pocket and turned to his dad. "Can you and Mom stay?"

Raymond didn't seem surprised. He only nodded and said, "Yeah, of course. You worried about something?"

Marcus pulled out the keys to his cruiser. "Two prisoners have escaped and could be headed this way. Warden says they're dangerous, so much so that he wants us to shoot first and ask questions later, so I don't want to leave Charlotte, Reine, and the kids alone."

He knew his dad understood. "Yeah, you got it," he said. "You be careful."

Marcus thumbed through his phone and pulled up the photos his wife had sent. One was dark skinned, the other lighter, both with dark hair and brown eyes, the same bugged-out mugshot expressions. Their names were Rafe Jackson and Holter Donnelly. "Charlotte, send these to Harold and Ryan, too," he called out over his shoulder as he opened the door, and his dad was right behind him, holding the inside screen. "Charlotte has the photos," Marcus told him. "Take a good look."

Raymond nodded. "I'll call Ryan and Owen," he said.

Marcus lingered just outside. He didn't know what to say to his dad. Out of anyone, he knew Raymond had a handle on this. "Thanks," he finally said, then started down the steps. He heard the door close behind him and the lock flick closed.

He dialed his cell phone, walking straight for his cruiser and climbing in. As he tossed his duty belt and coat on the passenger seat, the phone rang once, twice…

"Okay, what did you forget?" Suzanne answered. He thought he heard Arnie fussing in the background.

"Put Harold on," he said, shoving his cell phone in the mount on the dash. He started the car.

"No can do," Suzanne said. "He's in the shower. What is it?"

There she went, playing interference. He knew she was still pissed at him because he wouldn't let her play cop in his county.

"You tell Harold to get the hell out of the shower and call me back," he said. "There was a prison break. This is serious shit, Suzanne. Charlotte just sent him the photos and files. I need him to dig into it and then meet me at the office. I'm not messing around. Have him call me. Can you do that?"

She was quiet for a second. "Don't take my head off, Marcus. Yeah, I'll tell him. Hey, big brother?" She always seemed to need to have the last word.

"What?" he said as he backed the cruiser out, ready to get off the phone. He flicked on the headlights and gave the vehicle gas, looking out into the darkness, knowing he'd be taking a second and third look at anyone he saw that night, scrutinizing who they were and what they were doing.

"Watch your back," she said.

He felt a smile tug at the corners of his lips. "Always do," he said. "Now have Harold call me."

Marcus ended the call before his sister could add one more thing. As he rounded the corner, feeling his own angst, he drove slower than usual and took a good, long look at the few pickups parked along the street, scanning for anyone out walking. There was only a couple with a dog.

This was going to be a really long night.

"Lorhainne Eckhart is one of my go to authors when I want a guaranteed good book. So many twists and turns, but also so much love and such a strong sense of family."

(LORA W., REVIEWER)

New York Times & USA Today bestseller Lorhainne Eckhart is best known for writing Raw Relatable Real Romance where "Morals and family are running themes." As one fan calls her, she is the "Queen of the family saga." (aherman) writing "the ups and downs of what goes on within a family but also with some suspense, angst and of course a bit of romance thrown in for good measure." Follow Lorhainne on Bookbub to receive alerts on New Releases and Sales and join her mailing list at LorhainneEckhart.com for her Monday Blog, all book news, giveaways and FREE reads. With over 120 books, audiobooks, and multiple series published and available at all, retailers now translated into six languages. She is a multiple recipient of the Readers' Favorite Award for Suspense and Romance, and lives in the Pacific Northwest on an island, is the mother of three, her oldest has autism and she is an advocate for never giving up on your dreams.

"Lorhainne Eckhart has this uncanny way of just hitting the spot every time with her books."

(CAROLINE L., REVIEWER)

The O'Connells: *The O'Connells of Livingston, Montana are not your typical family. A riveting collection of stories surrounding the ups and downs of what goes on within a family but also with some suspense, angst and of course a bit of romance thrown in for good measure. "I thought I loved the Friessens, but I absolutely adore the O'Connell's. Each and every book has different genres of stories, but the one thing in common is how she is able to wrap it around the family, which is the heart of each story." (C. Logue)*

The Friessens: *An emotional big family*

romance series, the Friessen family siblings find their relationships tested, lay their hearts on the line, and discover lasting love! "Lorhainne Eckhart is one of my go to authors when I want a guaranteed good book. So many twists and turns, but also so much love and such a strong sense of family." (Lora W., Reviewer)

The Parker Sisters: The Parker Sisters are a close-knit family, and like any other family they have their ups and downs. Eckhart has crafted another intense family drama… "The character development is outstanding, and the emotional investment is high…" (Aherman, Reviewer)

The McCabe Brothers: Join the five McCabe siblings on their journeys to the dark and dangerous side of love! An intense, exhilarating collection of romantic thrillers you won't want to miss. — "Eckhart has a new series that is definitely worth the read. The queen of the family saga started this series with a spin-off of her wildly successful Friessen series." From a Readers' Favorite award—winning author and "queen of the family saga" (Aherman)

Lorhainne loves to hear from her readers! You can connect with me at:
www.LorhainneEckhart.com
lorhainneeckhart.le@gmail.com

In the Silence
In the Charm
Unexpected Consequences
It Was Always You
The First Time I Saw You
Welcome to My Arms
Welcome to Boston
I'll Always Love You
Ground Rules
A Reason to Breathe
You Are My Everything
Anything For You
The Homecoming
Stay Away From My Daughter
The Bad Boy
A Place of Our Own
The Visitor
All About Devon
Long Past Dawn
How to Heal a Heart
Keep Me In Your Heart

The O'Connells
The Neighbor
The Third Call
The Secret Husband
The Quiet Day
The Commitment
The Missing Father
The Hometown Hero
Justice
The Family Secret
The Fallen O'Connell

The Return of the O'Connells
And The She Was Gone
The Stalker
The O'Connell Family Christmas
The Girl Next Door
Broken Promises
The Gatekeeper
The Hunted

The McCabe Brothers
Don't Stop Me (Vic)
Don't Catch Me (Chase)
Don't Run From Me (Aaron)
Don't Hide From Me (Luc)
Don't Leave Me (Claudia)
Out of Time

A Billy Jo McCabe Mystery
Nothing As it Seems
Hiding in Plain Sight
The Cold Case
The Trap
Above the Law
The Stranger at the Door
The Children
The Last Stand
The Charity
The Sacrifice

The Wilde Brothers
The One (Joe and Margaret)
The Honeymoon, A Wilde Brothers Short
Friendly Fire (Logan and Julia)

Not Quite Married, A Wilde Brothers Short
A Matter of Trust (Ben and Carrie)
The Reckoning, A Wilde Brothers Christmas
Traded (Jake)
Unforgiven (Samuel)
The Holiday Bride

Married in Montana

His Promise
Love's Promise
A Promise of Forever

The Parker Sisters

Thrill of the Chase
The Dating Game
Play Hard to Get
What We Can't Have
Go Your Own Way
A June Wedding

Kate & Walker

One Night
Edge of Night
Last Night

Walk the Right Road Series

The Choice
Lost and Found
Merkaba
Bounty
Blown Away: The Final Chapter
He Came Back